The Billionaire Princess

CHRISTINA TETREAULT

Dedicated to My Friends Who Are Helping Me Through This Journey Called Parenthood and My Wonderful Beta Reader Donna Seger Kilroy

Chapter 1

Outside the window, the runway rapidly approached as the family jet touched down. No matter how many times Sara Sherbrooke traveled by plane it never ceased to amaze her how something so large could take off and land with such ease. As the plane rolled to a stop, she released the death grip she had on the armrests and checked her smartphone for any text messages before tossing it into her Coach bag and then waited for the plane door to open.

"Do you require any assistance, Ms. Sherbrooke?" Michelle, the private flight attendant for the jet, asked.

Sara moved toward the exit. "I'm fine, Michelle. I'll let you and Peter know when I'm ready to leave. When you are both done here go ahead and check into your hotel and enjoy yourselves."

Without waiting for an answer Sara walked down the stairs and out into the warm Hawaiian sun. As always it was a gorgeous day. It didn't seem like Hawaii ever had any other kind. At least every time she'd been here the weather was perfect and today seemed to be no different.

A few feet away Sara spotted the limo her brother Jake arranged and started toward it, her curiosity running rampant since yesterday when she'd received Jake's call insisting she come to Hawaii immediately with no explanation. She'd told him she had responsibilities and couldn't just up and leave without a good reason. All he said in response was to reschedule her meetings and then promised to have someone waiting for her at the airport.

"Once you're seated, I'll put your luggage in the trunk; we can leave once Mr. Hall arrives," the driver said opening the door for Sara.

At the mention of Jake's best friend and former college roommate, Sara's curiosity went into overdrive. Just what was her brother up to anyway?

Climbing into the car, Sara made herself comfortable and waited. The temptation to call Jake lurked in the back of her mind, but knowing her big brother the way she did, it would be pointless. When Jake was ready, he'd tell her what was going on and not a minute sooner.

As Sara sat sipping a bottle of sparkling water, the door opened again. Silently, she watched as Christopher Hall climbed in. If she hadn't seen him countless times on the web, she never would've recognized the man who'd climbed in the limo as her brother's Cal Tech roommate. She recalled meeting the tall skinny kid with shaggy light brown hair and glasses when her family moved Jake into his dorm freshman year. On the few occasions she had seen him back then he'd been dressed in jeans, Converse sneakers and t-shirts with hard-rock bands emblazoned on them. The man seated across from her now seemed to be someone else entirely.

Today his light brown hair was cut fashionably short and there was no sign of the glasses he used to wear. And those were not the only changes she noticed. There was no missing the way his broad shoulders filled out his dress shirt.

For a second Sara sat speechless and stared at the man, as her pulse kicked up a few notches. Before he noticed her staring, Sara regrouped and pasted on her best society smile. "Hi Christopher. Did Jake tell you what is going on?"

Christopher shook his head. "No. He just said to get out here, but I have a guess."

Sara expected him to continue and let her in on his suspicions. Instead he grabbed a soda water for himself. When several minutes passed and he didn't say anything else, she couldn't keep herself from asking her next question, "So, what is your guess?"

Christopher paused with the bottle halfway to his mouth. "My money is on a wedding, but it's just a guess."

"A wedding? No. Charlie and Jake wouldn't do that. Our parents would be furious."

"Like I said it's just a guess, but I know Jake and an out-of-the-blue wedding wouldn't surprise me at all."

Would her brother do that to their parents? Sure a sudden unexpected wedding might be something Jake would talk about, but not something he'd ever go through with. Jake Sherbrooke and Charlotte O'Brien's wedding would be a huge affair much like Dylan and Callie's the year before. Considering the size of the Sherbrooke family and the fact that the American public seemed so fascinated by them, how could it be anything less?

But if not a wedding like Christopher predicted, what other reason could Jake have for asking Christopher and her to Hawaii on such short notice? Other than an impromptu wedding like Christopher suggested nothing else made any sense.

"Have you meet Charlie?" Sara asked in an attempt to start a conversation. Over the years they'd had few conversations so Sara figured she could either ask him about his company or the one thing they had in common, her brother.

Christopher returned his water to the holder near the door and Sara's eyes watched the way the muscles in his upper arm flexed and moved. The sight sent her hand toward the air vent, which she redirected toward her face.

"I meet her last year at Jake's office and we've all gotten together several times since. I like her. She seems perfect for him."

"I think so too." Sara reached for more water. "She's definitely the right woman for my brother." She took a sip from the bottle and then asked him about his company.

About twenty minutes after leaving the airport, the limo arrived at The Sherbrooke Resort and Spa, one of Sherbrooke Enterprises's finest hotels in Maui. Upon entering the resort Christopher and Sara crossed the lobby to the private elevator behind the hotel concierge's desk and in silence they rode the elevator up to the penthouse apartment, which occupied the entire 21st floor. When the doors opened they walked directly into the living room.

"Good, you two are here. Everyone else is out on the balcony." Jake crossed the room toward them.

Sara dropped her Coach bag onto a nearby table and embraced her older brother. "Care to tell us what's going on?" Before letting go she dropped a kiss on Jake's cheek.

With a devilish smile Jake moved toward Christopher and slapped him on the back. "Why don't you both come outside and join everyone. Then I'll tell you what's up."

"Who else is here?" Sara fell into step alongside Jake and Christopher.

"Charlie, of course, Maureen, Callie and Dylan." He didn't wait for a response before stepping onto the balcony that ran the entire length of the building.

Immediately, Sara thought of Christopher's remark in the car about a wedding. His guess must be right. What other reason could they have for inviting Charlie's mom?

While Jake walked over to his fiancée, Sara took a seat near Dylan and Callie.

They sat on an extra-wide padded lounge chair. Dylan's arm rested across Callie's shoulders and their hands were clasped together. Sara fought hard to suppress an eye roll in their direction. Since meeting Callie, her no-nonsense workaholic half-brother had become quite the romantic.

"So are you going to tell us what's up or should we guess?" Christopher asked the very question on her mind.

"Charlie and I are getting married tonight."

"You'd better be joking or Mom's going to kill you!" Sara looked from Charlie to Jake waiting for one of them to answer her.

"I'm not joking. Dylan and Callie helped us arrange everything. We getting married tonight at five o'clock."

Even though her brother and his fiancée had been engaged since New Year's Eve they hadn't set a wedding date or to her knowledge even started to make formal plans. She guessed they were in no rush.

"What about Mom and Dad?" Sara glanced around at the other people present. No one but Maureen seemed the least bit surprised by Jake's announcement.

"They don't know. And we want to keep it that way," Jake answered.

"Have you lost your mind?" Sara came to her feet. "You cannot get married without them here, Jake. Mom will never forgive you." She knew her brother liked to do things his own way, but she never thought he'd go this far.

In response Jake gave a slight shrug. "It's not about them. Charlie and I don't want a huge affair like Callie and Dylan. That's not us."

Sara couldn't argue with him on that point. She did find it hard to picture Jake and Charlie having such an elaborate and formal wedding. That didn't mean she couldn't see them having something grander than this. And not to have their parents there felt wrong.

"If Mom knew about this she'd insist on making it a big event and then the media would descend. We don't want that. She'll be angry, but eventually she'll get over it."

The way she saw it, saying their parents would be upset was the understatement of the century. At the same time though, she couldn't disagree with her brother that Elizabeth Sherbrooke would insist on turning the wedding into a grand event for the whole world to see.

"I still think that you're crazy." Sara looked over at Callie and Dylan who had remained silent so far. "And why didn't you tell me about this Dylan, if you both knew." It hurt to think Jake trusted them with the secret but not her.

"Need to know. He needed me to help arrange things. Otherwise he wouldn't have told us either," Dylan answered. "We didn't say anything because we figured the less that people knew, the less likely someone would slip. And it's not like it's been planned for long. We finalized things about three weeks ago."

Dylan's answer made her feel a little better, but not much. She knew how to keep a secret. Their plans would've been just as safe with her. "When do you plan to tell Mom and Dad? I might make plans to be out of the country when you do."

Jake laughed. "I'll warn you before I do. But since they are leaving the country tomorrow it'll be a while."

Christopher watched the exchange between his best friend and the other guests. Jake's announcement hadn't surprised him in the least. Actually, he'd expected something like this since Jake had told him about the engagement. An impromptu wedding near the beach fit the couple in question perfectly. But, judging by their expressions, Charlie's mom and Jake's sister hadn't expected anything like this.

As Sara and Jake discussed their parents, Christopher tuned out the words and watched the emotions on Sara's face, unable to tear his eyes from her. No one could deny that she was an amazingly beautiful woman.

He'd thought the same thing the first time he'd met her his freshman year at Cal Tech. She'd accompanied her parents when Jake moved in, and when she walked into their dorm room, he thought he was seeing a living angel. Even at sixteen, she'd taken his breath away. Not that she noticed him though. At eighteen he'd been tall and lanky, and his personal grooming had ranked low on his priority list. Thanks to the gym and Jake's help, his appearance had drastically changed in the years since they first met. Today no one would recognize him as the geek from Wisconsin and not just because of the changes to his outward appearance.

Sara had changed as well. She'd gone from a beautiful sixteen year old to a gorgeous woman. Though being his best friend's sister meant she was off limits to him. Still, that didn't mean he couldn't admire her from afar. He suspected few men could be in her presence without drooling all over themselves.

"I doubt this surprises you."

Jake's voice broke into Christopher's thoughts and he found himself grateful that his dark sunglasses concealed his eyes. "Not at all. I just thought you'd do it sooner. I told Sara on the ride here I thought we were going to a wedding."

"And she disagreed. What was her theory?" Jake asked with a hint of laughter in his voice.

"She didn't have one or if she did she kept it to herself." Christopher let his eyes travel back to Sara. "But this suits the two of you."

"Thanks for coming." Jake slapped him on the back. "It means a lot to me."

"Hey, I figured if my guess was right I couldn't miss seeing Prince Charming himself get married," Christopher answered, making reference to the title the media had given Jake years before. "Besides, when my sisters hear that you got married they are going to want all the details."

Jake opened his mouth to speak, but Christopher beat him to it. "Don't worry I won't tell them anything until it goes public. If I told them, it would be all over the Internet in an hour."

Jake nodded his appreciation. "I don't think you've meet Maureen. I'll introduce you."

Christopher glanced over at the older woman who was now in a conversation with Charlie and Sara. In silence he and Jake crossed the rooftop to where the three women stood.

"Maureen, I'd like you to meet Christopher Hall," Jake said interrupting.

A wide friendly smile crossed Maureen's face. "You must be Jake's college roommate Charlie told me about. It's nice to meet you." Maureen extended her hand.

"Nice to meet you too. Jake tells me you make the best apple pie he's ever tasted." Christopher extended his hand toward the older woman.

Christopher and the others remained outside. After lunch Christopher retreated to his own bedroom. In addition to having a private elevator, the penthouse apartment had a full kitchen, living room, five bedrooms, and access to a private rooftop pool. During lunch he'd received several text messages from work and he wanted to handle them before the ceremony began.

A few hours later Sara stood between Christopher and Maureen, as Judge Fallon began the wedding ceremony on the deserted beach just feet away from the rolling waves. Sara had to admit the setting of the ceremony fit her brother and Charlie to a T. They both adored the ocean and spent as much time as possible out on Jake's sailboat. The entire feel of the ceremony, in fact, fit the couple. It was low key and informal. There was no over-the-top wedding gown or a tux with tails. And while the ceremony fit the couple beautifully it was far from what she dreamed of having some day, assuming that day ever came. With each failed relationship, Sara began to doubt more and more that she'd ever find the right man. So far she'd managed to find herself attracted to men who only saw her last name—a name with the right business and political connections.

Without intending to, Sara sighed, drawing Christopher's attention. For a moment his dark chocolate brown eyes studied her face and her heartbeat sped up. After a second or two he looked away, and Sara's heartbeat returned to normal.

Did her brothers know how lucky they both were? They'd both found their perfect matches and neither woman expected anything in return. Although she'd never told Callie or Charlie, she admired them for that. They were both able to see her brothers for the men they were on the inside. Not many people seemed able to do that. At least not many of the ones she'd met.

In front of her, Jake pulled Charlie into his arms and kissed her, signaling the end of the short civil ceremony. Next to her Charlie's mom wept. Without a second thought, Sara wrapped an arm around the older woman's shoulder.

"Are you okay?" she asked, wishing she had a few tissues on hand.

Maureen nodded and wiped at the tears sliding down her cheek. "I just can't believe my baby girl is married. I'll be fine. Go on and join the others." Maureen patted her on the arm and motioned to the others with her head.

Sara hesitated for a second but then moved forward to join the others as they congratulated the happy couple. She listened as both Callie and Dylan welcomed Charlie to the family and then turned to Jake. As children, with only a two-year difference between them, they'd always been close. They had grown apart a bit through the years, since they'd both been sent off to different boarding schools. Yet she still considered him one of her closest friends, the one person she could trust no matter what. So before anyone else could approach him, she moved in and hugged him.

"Congratulations," she said before dropping a kiss on his cheek. "But I still think you're nuts for not inviting Mom and Dad." She couldn't stop herself from adding the last part.

"I'll deal with them later. Besides now they can make an even bigger deal of your wedding when the time comes."

Sara merely shook her head in response. Her brother never cared what their parents thought. Sometimes she envied him for that. "That's more like *if* rather than *when*, Jake." She tried to hide the sarcasm from her voice.

"You're wrong. You'll see. I promise," he said in his annoying big-brother-knows-all tone.

""I'm not going to argue with you on your wedding day." She gave him another hug and moved away before he could offer anymore brotherly wisdom, something he loved to do. He insisted it was his job as her older brother, but she suspected it had more to do with wanting to annoy her.

Whatever the reason, she really didn't want to discuss that particular topic any further. It'd only put her in a bad mood, and she didn't want to ruin the day for her brother and Charlie. Instead she moved toward the bride to congratulate her.

Although Jake and Charlie had been together for almost a year now, Sara didn't know her that well. Charlie and Jake lived in Virginia, while she lived in DC, which should've made visiting easy. But, Charlie was a doctor, and her schedule didn't fit well with Sara's hectic schedule on the Hill.

"Congratulations, Charlie. You look gorgeous." Sara stepped in front of Charlie and hugged her. Today Charlie wore a simple but elegant white gown that ended just above the knee. Her red hair was pulled up with a simple silver comb holding it in place. A simple white gold necklace with an emerald pendant hung around her neck and matching emerald earrings hung from her ears.

Charlie's face beamed with happiness as Sara pulled back. "Thank you. I'm glad you came. Jake was worried you wouldn't make it on such short notice."

"I wouldn't have missed this for the world." Even if she'd been on the other side of the planet, she would've found a way to get to Hawaii when Jake asked her. "Are you two going on a honeymoon?"

"We're spending a few days here, but then I need to get back. In the fall we're going to Scotland and England."

Both were beautiful countries she'd visited many times, but neither were places she'd pick for a honeymoon. "You're going to keep working at the hospital?" Charlie had retired from the Navy and taken a position at a hospital in Virginia the previous fall.

"I love it there, so I see no reason to leave."

Sara mentally nodded in approval. She already knew that Charlie loved her brother and not his money or powerful family name, still Charlie's decision to stay at the hospital further reassured her.

If only she could find a man who'd look past all that too. It seemed as if every man she dated saw her as a dollar sign rather than a flesh-and-blood woman. Perhaps men weren't capable of seeing beyond money and power. After all, the only two people she knew who truly didn't seem to care about those things were Charlie and Callie. Neither had been drawn to their spouses because of material goods. Maybe only women could look beyond what someone had and see the real person, though both of her brothers had dated their share of gold diggers before meeting their spouses.

While Sara pondered the differences between men and women, Charlie told her about why they'd chosen Scotland and England for a honeymoon rather than somewhere more exotic. As she did, the skin on the back of Sara's neck tingled. At first she dismissed the sensation. When it didn't go away she shot a quick glance over Charlie's shoulder, but it revealed nothing out of the ordinary. A large portion of the beach had been closed off to other guests, and any people on the beach were much further down. So far down in fact, she doubted they would be able to tell who had just gotten married.

Still the feeling remained.

Automatically, Sara nodded in response to Charlie's words as she looked over toward her brother, her eyes locking with Christopher's. For a second or two their eyes stayed connected, his expression unreadable.

What did he see when he looked at her? Did he see the daddy's-little-princess that many of Jake's other friends imagined her to be? Did he see her as some political pawn like her last boyfriend? Breaking contact, she focused back on Charlie and their conversation.

Since she first met Charlie at Dylan and Callie's wedding the year before, she'd tried not to make the same mistakes with her that she'd made with Callie when they'd first met.

"Your brother couldn't come too?" Sara asked. She knew Charlie had an older brother although she'd never met him.

"We invited him but the Victorian Rose expected guests this weekend. He didn't want to cancel those reservations. Jake offered to compensate him for the loss, but Sean insisted canceling at the last minute would be bad for business."

Sara nodded, a negative review on a website somewhere could ruin a small bed and breakfast.

"Ma will tell him all about the wedding when she gets home, and we're visiting them in two weeks."

Christopher walked through the glass doors separating the living room area of the penthouse apartment from the rooftop pool. *Callie must have planned this.*

Charlie was a terrific woman and a perfect match for Jake, yet, she didn't strike him as the romantic type. And while Jake had always been smooth with the ladies, this didn't look like something he'd come up with either. Vases filled with long stemmed red and white roses sat on every table. Candles placed along the edge of the rooftop near the railing flickered as did the candles floating in the pool. The padded lounges had been pushed together and covered so they resembled wide couches, and throw pillows had been added to increase the effect. Soft music played in the background, loud enough for dancing but not so loud you couldn't have a conversation. A slight breeze from the ocean kept the rooftop a comfortable temperature as the wedding guests mingled over drinks and food.

Before joining the others, he stopped at the bar, which had been set up in the far corner, and ordered a vodka martini then filled a plate from the buffet. Satisfied with his food selections, he joined Jake and his family.

"Congratulations again," Christopher said sitting in an empty seat facing the glass door. "Who did all this? I know it wasn't Jake." With his hand he gestured around the rooftop.

Jake nodded in Callie's direction. "Callie planned the reception and Dylan arranged everything else."

"Nicely done." He looked over at Callie who sat diagonally across the table next to Dylan and Maureen. "Aren't we one short?" Christopher asked noticing that Sara still hadn't joined them. In fact he hadn't seen her since the photographer finished the pictures on the beach.

Jake paused with his wine glass almost to his mouth, "She needed to return some phone calls."

The sound of the glass door sliding on its runner caught Christopher's attention, and he immediately looked up. He watched Sara step outside and close the door behind her. She still wore the turquoise sundress from the wedding, but now her blonde hair hung in thick waves skimming her shoulders.

Raising his fork to his mouth, he watched as she crossed to the bar and ordered herself a drink. She moved with such grace and elegance—even if he hadn't known who she was, he would've known she wasn't just some ordinary woman. Everything about her spoke of wealth and privilege.

Since no one else seemed to notice, he kept his gaze locked on her as she stopped for food before joining the table.

"Sorry that took so long." Sara pulled out a chair across from him.

"We know you just like to make an entrance," Jake joked, pushing his empty plate away from him. Immediately a waitress appeared to clear the dish away.

Sara made a childish face and stuck her tongue out at her brother causing Christopher to nearly choke on the carrot he'd swallowed. While he could easily picture one of his sisters doing the exact same thing to him, the action didn't fit with the image he had of the proper and elegant Sara Sherbrooke. But if anyone else found her behavior odd, no one commented. Jake simply laughed and pushed his chair back.

"How about a dance, Mrs. Sherbrooke?" he asked holding out a hand to Charlie. Without a word Charlie accepted, and the couple moved toward the other side of the pool.

The sound of a chair scratching on the ground drew Christopher's attention to Dylan whispering something in Callie's ear before they both stood and joined the dancing couple. Shortly after that Maureen pushed her chair back as well.

"I think I'll say goodnight. It's already tomorrow morning back in North Salem."

Left alone at the table, Sara and Christopher ordered another round of drinks and finished their dinner in silence while the other two couples danced to the slow love songs pouring from the speakers.

Finished with dinner Christopher leaned back in his chair and watched Sara from across the table. Since joining the party she hadn't said much beyond the basic pleasantries.

"Do you want to dance?" he asked before taking the last sip of his second martini.

She was watching the two couples moving to the music and immediately her head whipped around to face him, but Sara remained silent.

"If you don't want to that's fine too." It didn't matter much to him either way. When it came to dancing he usually avoided it. Yet she'd been watching the other couples with such longing, he guessed she enjoyed it.

Sara started to push her chair back. "Sure."

Christopher followed her toward the dance floor. When she stopped and faced him, he encircled her waist with his arms and pulled her closer but kept an appropriate distance between them.

Once Sara slid her arms around his neck, they began to move to the classic love ballad pouring from the speakers. Slowly one song melded into another, and soon he couldn't remember how long they'd danced or when he'd pulled her so close. No space remained between them as they moved as one with her head resting against his chest. But he didn't mind, in fact he liked the way her body felt pressed up against his. He didn't even mind that every now and then a strand of her silky hair blew across his face.

Throughout their dancing, his eyes strayed back to the woman in his arms.

He enjoyed watching the candlelight flicker across her skin, and the way she felt in his arms.

A few feet away Charlie and Jake danced and, as the song ended, he noticed Charlie whisper in Jake's ear.

"I'm told it's time to call it a night. We'll see you all tomorrow." The smile on Jake's face told everyone he was more than happy to head inside.

"I doubt that," Dylan said from near the pool where he and Callie danced.

Jake ignored his half-brother and kept on walking.

Christopher agreed with Dylan. He'd be surprised if he saw Jake or Charlie again before he returned home.

"I think it's time we went inside too. We'll see you two sometime tomorrow." Dylan led Callie toward the glass doors.

Christopher paused for a moment even though a new song started. "Looks like we've been deserted," he said letting his eyes rest on Sara's face.

Sara met his gaze and then nodded, "Seems that way."

Without any warning, Sara moved out of his arms. "I think I need another drink."

He couldn't be certain but he thought he detected the slightest hint of embarrassment in her voice. "Sounds like a good idea. What can I make for you?"

"Another Cosmo would be great," she answered with a tiny half smile.

Nodding he headed toward the vacant bar. He'd never received any formal training, but he knew how to mix the staple drinks. Once both drinks were prepared he carried them to Sara, standing near the pool.

For a while they both stood in silence gazing out at the beach below. Although long past sunset, the lights from the other hotels and the streets below provided enough illumination to see the sandy beach and rolling waves.

"Are you working for Sherbrooke Enterprises now?" He remembered Jake telling him Sara graduated from Harvard Law School. A position in the company's legal department seemed the next logical step for her. Assuming she worked at all. She didn't have any reason to.

"No. I'm Senator David Healy's chief of staff. I've been with him since his campaign."

She took a large swallow of her drink and he watched, mesmerized for some reason by the way she held her glass to her lips. The urge to pull the glass away and replace it with his mouth started to overtake him. It wasn't the first time since meeting her years before that he'd been physically attracted to her, any man with a pulse would be. But tonight the pull was stronger. Different somehow. In a way he couldn't explain.

"You look surprised," Sara said reminding Christopher that he still hadn't responded.

"I don't associate beautiful woman with politics." He didn't stop to filter the thoughts flowing through his head and the words spilled out.

Countless men had called her beautiful, yet coming from him it sounded different, more sincere perhaps. Running her tongue over her lips to moisten them, she met his gaze. Then they both took a step forward at the same instant. A tiny part of her brain went on autopilot when she felt her body come into contact with his. Slowly, he lowered his head toward hers and she found herself craving the taste of his lips more than she craved her next breath.

When his lips settled on hers he placed his hands on her shoulders, warmth seeping though her body. Their kiss remained gentle and sweet, but Sara allowed herself to learn the taste and texture of his lips, something she'd wanted to do since he climbed into the limo that afternoon.

The desire to increase the intensity of the kiss soon exploded. Sara wrapped her arms around Christopher's waist and anchored him against her as they continued to kiss. When the need for air became so great she feared his lungs would explode, Christopher pulled his mouth away from hers and began to leave a trail of kisses from the corner of her mouth across her jaw and down her neck.

In response Sara tilted her neck to the side to give him better access. Christopher continued his trail of kisses as his hands slid up and down the skin of her uncovered back causing her to tingle at his touch.

"Maybe we should go inside," he whispered near her ear.

She nodded in agreement without pausing to consider the ramifications. Moving on autopilot, she let him lead her back inside to his room as his hands and lips stayed in contact with her body.

After closing the door with his foot, she heard him lock it. One hand gripped her hip making it difficult to move, while he attempted to unbutton his shirt with the other. When the buttons wouldn't cooperate fast enough he yanked at the front tearing the buttons off and sending them in every direction. Once his shirt no longer remained as a barrier between them, he reached for her zipper. In the back of her mind, she expected him stop at any second—for him to come to his senses, pull away and toss her from the room. Instead he slid the zipper down her back and then pushed the thin straps from her shoulders, making the dress fall in a puddle around her feet.

Kicking the dress aside, she reached for his belt buckle. As her hands worked to undo it, his hands explored the contours of her back only stopping once to unclasp on her strapless bra.

When they'd both managed to dispose of each other's clothing, he moved them, stopping when the backs of her legs hit the bed. Then in one final movement they tumbled onto the bed together.

Chapter 2

Sara awoke and was instantly aware of two things; she had no clothes on and there was an arm draped across her stomach that didn't belong to her. As the cobwebs of sleep cleared from her mind bits and pieces from the night before came trickling back into her consciousness.

After the ceremony everyone had gathered for dinner and dancing. At some point everyone but she and Christopher disappeared from the romantic poolside setting and she had yet another cosmo, her fourth of the night. Normally she stopped after two. She could only remember one occasion when she'd consumed three and she didn't know why she had so many the night before.

After the drink they'd kissed. At first the kiss had been gentle, but it'd changed as desire and longing surged through her veins. It'd been more than two years since a man kissed her. Without any warning her body instantly responded. Soon she and Christopher were holding onto each other for dear life as they made their way to his room.

Not once had she paused to think about what she was doing. She'd let him take her dress off without any protest. She thought she remembered helping him remove an article or two of his clothing, but she couldn't be certain.

Groaning at the memory, she squeezed her eyes together. Maybe if she didn't open them all these memories would turn out to be just part of a dream. A very nice dream, but one she'd didn't want to be real. Maybe the weight she felt across her middle was a figment of her imagination.

Sara shifted her leg a little and the feel of crisp hairs against her leg dashed away any hope that she was still dreaming. Slowly taking in a deep breath and then exhaling, Sara opened her eyes.

Something between a groan and a laugh bubbled up and out of her when her eyes settled on Christopher's face. His eyes were still closed and his breathing remained even, as if he didn't have a care in the world.

Hell, what was I thinking? She'd never in her life had a one-night stand. Not to mention this was her brother's best friend. *How was she going to face Christopher now? What about her brother?* She'd die if Jake ever found out.

Could she sneak out before he woke up? While it might not solve the overall problem at hand, at least she would not have to face him naked the minute he woke up.

In an effort not to wake him, Sara slid toward the edge of the bed all the while keeping her eyes locked on his face. *Almost there.*

The arm Christopher had draped across her stomach slipped off. With one leg over the side of the bed, she sat up prepared to retrieve her dress and yank it on.

"Sara?"   Christopher sounded as confused as she'd been when she first woke up.

Embarrassed by her state of undress and unable to get her dress without standing, she yanked the sheet around her.

For what felt like an eternity a heavy silence hung in the air between them. "I... we... uh... should talk."

The mattress shifted and she knew without looking that he'd pulled himself into a sitting position.

"I'm... I didn't intend for this to happen," Christopher said, his tone apologetic.

He took hold of her hand and heat flooded her face. Unable to look at him, she nodded, not sure whether to tell him she understood or tell him it was okay. At the moment a whole plethora of perplexing emotions churned inside her.

"Sara?"

Since she couldn't undo the events from the night before, she had to face them. "We're both adults. Last night happened. No big deal." Sara struggled to keep her voice sounding nonchalant. "Trust me, things like this happen all the time. I don't even know how many times it happened during the eighteen months I worked on the senator's campaign," she said matter-of-factly. *Just not to me.* "People get lonely and when they do they look for companionship." Did her argument sound better to him than it did to her? She hoped so.

"Still it shouldn't have happened. I'm sorry."

She saw worry and guilt in his eyes when she looked over at him. Placing a hand on his bare shoulder, she leaned a little closer. "You have nothing to apologize for, okay? Let's pretend it never happened." Could she do that? Saying the words was one thing, carrying them out another.

"I should go before anyone gets up and sees me leaving." Sara dropped her hand. The way she saw it, if she left now she had more than a fifty-fifty chance of getting back to her room unseen by either of her brothers. "If it's all the same to you, I'd rather keep this a secret between us."

Sara knew she didn't imagine the look of relief that washed across his face.

"You read my mind. Jake would kill me if he found out," Christopher answered, his face devoid of any humor. In one fluid movement he swung his legs over the side of the bed so he faced away from her. "Go ahead and get dressed. I promise not to look."

She glanced once at his bare back. The night before she hadn't seen any of it, but her hands had roamed across every inch. In the morning light she could see the muscles her hands had traced the night before and immediately her hands tingled wanting to do so again.

Bad idea. Very bad idea. Before she could give in to her hands' desire, she jumped off the bed and snatched up her dress. In record time the dress went over her head, and she zipped it up. While her first instinct was to fly out the bedroom door, she paused long enough to open it and peek into the hall. From there the coast appeared clear.

Please let me make it to my room. "I'll see you later," she said without looking back at Christopher. Sara didn't stick around for his reply. Slipping into the hall, she closed the door gently behind her.

So far so good. Sara walked down the hall toward an empty living room. The curtains covering the windows and French doors remained closed, hinting at the fact no one else was up yet. As she crossed the living room toward the hall leading to her room, she held her breath. Just a few more steps and their secret would be safe. No one would ever know.

Feeling a bit like a criminal sneaking into somewhere she didn't belong, Sara walked into her room and closed the door. Exhaling the breath she'd been holding, she leaned back against the bedroom door. She'd made it. Their secret was safe.

Two hours later Sara stood at her bathroom sink. She knew someone was up, she'd heard voices but she'd remained locked in her room. How could she ever face Christopher again? Or Jake? Yeah, sure Jake knew she wasn't a virgin, but that didn't mean he wanted her sleeping with his best friend either.

And she didn't want to imagine how Christopher must see her now. What kind of woman had a one-night stand with her brother's best friend? Not someone like her. At least not before last night. Somehow though, she hadn't been able to help herself. For more than two years, she'd stayed clear of men, content with building a name for herself in politics. Then in a matter of hours, she'd gone from simply dancing to waking up next to a complete stranger, naked.

Okay, maybe not a complete stranger, she reasoned. Still they didn't know each other that well. Prior to this weekend, she couldn't even remember the last time they'd seen each other.

I cannot stay in here all day. Even if she didn't come out for any other reason, at some point she needed to eat. At the thought of food her stomach rumbled. *Come on. You're a Sherbrooke. Sherbrookes don't hide.*

After one last glance in the mirror, Sara marched out into the living room only to find it empty. The sound of movement in the kitchen told her someone was nearby.

The barest hint of cinnamon mixed with the aroma of coffee tickled her nose when she walked into the fully functional kitchen where Maureen O'Brien sat with a steaming coffee mug in front of her.

"You must have stayed up late last night," Maureen said after greeting her. "I just finished breakfast, but I can make you something. Dylan and Christopher ate all the French toast I made, but I can make more if you want that."

Before she could stop herself, Sara looked around again for either of the two men. "Where is everyone?" she asked even though she only cared about the current location of one particular individual.

"Dylan and Callie went to the beach. Christopher left for the airport about an hour ago. Jake and Charlie are still in bed."

Jake and Charlie were still in bed, no big surprise there. They'd gotten married yesterday. As for Dylan and Callie, it made sense that they'd gone to the beach. Both enjoyed it, but didn't get there often, living in the city. Christopher's departure though seemed odd. It didn't seem like him to leave so abruptly. Then again what did she know? With the exception of the previous night's activities, she'd never spent more than an hour with him at a time.

"Don't worry about it, Maureen. I'll call for something." While the penthouse apartment in the hotel had a complete kitchen, it also had full access to the hotel's amenities, which included two five-star restaurants.

"That's silly. Let me make you something," Maureen said waving her hand for added emphasis.

The French toast and coffee from earlier did smell delicious, and Jake had told her what an excellent cook Maureen was. "If you really don't mind, some of that French toast would be great."

As Maureen cooked she chatted away about the wedding the day before and Hawaii in general. Sara was grateful that the woman didn't mind that she did little more than nod in agreement. At the moment she couldn't handle an in-depth conversation with anyone. All her thoughts remained centered on the previous night's events. The fact that she'd slept with Christopher seemed like a dream or a scene out of a movie. She'd avoided men for two years yet after a few drinks and a single kiss she'd lost all of her common sense and her dress. How was she going to face her brother? No matter what, she couldn't let him find out. Who knew how it might affect his friendship with Christopher?

"I wish they'd invited your parents," Maureen said. She placed a plate piled high with slices of French toast in front of her. "They should've been here." Maureen sat down across from her. "Your mom will be heartbroken."

Sara nodded in agreement and reached for the maple syrup. Heartbroken wasn't the only adjective that came to mind. Furious also ranked up there. Her father wouldn't be pleased either, but he would understand far better than their mother.

"I'm glad I'm not the one who has to tell them," Sara said.

"Tell who what?" Jake asked walking toward the table. "Is that French toast I smell?"

The hunger she'd felt a few seconds earlier disappeared at the sound of Jake's voice. "Tell Mom and Dad you got married." She kept her eyes on her breakfast when she answered. If she looked at her brother now, she feared he'd know something wasn't right. While he'd never guess the true cause of her unease, he'd hound her until he got the information from her.

"They'll understand eventually." He took a seat on the other side of the table. "Where is everyone else?"

"Callie and Dylan headed to the beach and your friend Christopher left for the airport after breakfast," Maureen answered, placing a plate piled high with slices of French toast on the table.

"Left? I wonder why? I figured he'd stick around for the weekend." Jake dug into his breakfast with gusto.

Sara kept her eyes down. "Probably business. You didn't exactly give anyone time to plan for being away from work."

"Sometimes it's fun to be spontaneous, Sara. Admit it, even you had fun yesterday."

A flicker of apprehension coursed through her as the memories from the night before blossomed in her mind. "I guess." She popped a piece of French toast in her mouth and hoped Jake would change the subject. She didn't want to discuss the events of last night with anyone, ever.

Sara finished a portion of her breakfast and then stood. "Maureen, that was delicious, but I cannot eat another bite." She picked up her plate, prepared to carry it into the kitchen.

"I'll finish it up for you."

Sara shook her head. She didn't know where he put it all. "It's all yours." She passed the plate to him. "I'm going to read my emails."

Her beeping phone on the desk greeted her when she re-entered her room.

Picking it up she saw one text message from a number she didn't recognize. *Thought you'd be more comfortable if I wasn't around when you got up,* the message read.

That caused an unidentified emotion to wash over her, and she hit delete. No one could ever see that message.

Chapter 3

Christopher immediately recognized the ringtone coming from his phone. Everyone in his contact list from his mother to his housekeeper had their own distinct ring.

For half a heartbeat he considered answering, but then he hit ignore and let the call from Jake go straight to voicemail. They hadn't spoken in almost three weeks. Not because Jake hadn't called, but rather because Christopher had been avoiding all communication with him.

Dropping the phone onto his desk, he turned his attention back to his computer screen. Despite his efforts to concentrate, he couldn't shake the guilt and shame eating away at his conscience in a way he'd never experienced before.

He considered Jake Sherbrooke one of his closest friends. In all the time they'd known each other, Jake had never treated him as anything other than an equal, even early in their friendship when he'd been nothing but a Cal Tech freshman from a small town in Wisconsin on a full academic scholarship. And how had he repaid him? By breaking the one unspoken rule between men—sleeping with your best friend's little sister. Admiring Sara from afar was one thing, but he'd gone way beyond that. While she brushed the whole incident off as no big deal, it was a huge deal to him. And now that it had happened he didn't know how he'd ever face his friend again. Until he was confident he could talk to Jake without blurting out the truth, he figured it best to avoid him all together.

Christopher reread the line on the computer screen and prepared to finish the document, only to be interrupted by a knock on his office door.

"Yes," he said, annoyance at the interruption slipping into his voice.

"I'm working on your calendar for next week before I leave," Caroline—his sister and executive assistant—said, walking into the room. "Do you plan to attend the literacy fundraiser Senator Healy's wife is co-sponsoring next week?"

With everything else, he'd forgotton all about the invitation he'd received from David Healy. While he received similar invites all the time, this one had been made in person when he'd run into David weeks earlier. During a round of golf they'd started discussing Christopher's company and how he might be able to assist with a new education initiative David had helped prepare, which was to be voted on soon. When the game ended, he'd invited Christopher to the fundraiser being held in Rhode Island. At the time he'd said maybe, but hadn't thought about it since that afternoon.

Sara worked as David's chief of staff, which meant she might be in attendance. His pulse raced at the thought of seeing her again. Since she'd walked out of his bedroom, he'd thought about her frequently. That morning he'd forced himself to leave Hawaii before either she or Jake got up. While part of him had wanted to stay as far away from her as possible, another part couldn't help but want to see her.

Several times since then he'd picked up his phone, intent on calling her. Unfortunately he couldn't come up with a good reason to do so. The fundraiser was both a blessing and a curse. It gave him the perfect excuse to see her. At the same time though he feared what would happen when he did.

Only one way to find out. "Thanks for reminding me. Yes, I plan on going."

Caroline's fingers moved over the tablet in her hand. "Do you want to leave that morning or the day before? Right now you have nothing scheduled for the day before."

"Tell Jim to be ready to fly the day before." A full day to adjust to the time difference between the West coast and the East coast would be useful.

❦

Sara accepted the glass of Pinot Noir from the waiter and took a sip while Mia Troy spoke. Although the actress spent her days in Hollywood now, she had strong ties to New England. Like Sara she'd been born there and had attended Harvard University for a short time before moving to California to pursue an acting career. Since then she'd become a vocal political advocate supporting many politicians, including President Sherbrooke.

"If I was going to be here longer, I'd say we should have a girls' night out," Mia said, sounding as if the idea had just come to her.

Although she didn't intend to stay in Rhode Island long, the idea of a girls' night out sounded nice. She couldn't remember the last time she'd gone out with some girlfriends. Part of the reason was her job. During the senator's campaign, she'd kept her mind focused on getting him elected. Now that he was in office, it was her responsibility to make sure everything ran smoothly and that he eventually got re-elected. With all that, there wasn't a lot of time for socializing.

Sara couldn't place all the blame for her nonexistent social life on her job though. She had free time, but chose to avoid society. Even before Phillip Young entered her life she'd known people sometimes associated with her only because of her last name. Thanks to her relationship with Phillip though, that fact was branded on her mind and, as a result, she now distanced herself from people, both men and women.

"I'm leaving in the morning, though," Mia said. "I'm expected in Rome on Saturday for the start of a new movie."

"Some other time maybe," Sara said, her voice the right combination of disappointment and understanding.

Not long after, Mia excused herself, leaving Sara alone for the first time all evening. Since she had entered the ballroom hours earlier, she'd been surrounded by people. Some she'd known for years, while others she'd only met after she started working with the senator. And while she shouldn't feel alone in such a crowded room, she did. Put in the same situation a month earlier and she'd feel at ease. Ready to mix and socialize with everyone there. Politics was in her blood. However, since her brother's wedding, she'd been thinking about the one thing both her brothers had but she didn't. Someone to love and who loved her in return regardless of anything else.

Tonight's all about politics and money. Don't forget that. And a big part of politics was socializing so right now she needed to do some of that.

"I hoped to see you here tonight."

Sara froze in her tracks. She hadn't heard his voice in more than two years, but she recognized it immediately. Phillip. Before turning around, she slowly counted to ten. "I'm Senator Healy's chief of staff, so it's expected." She forced herself to use a courteous tone, even though more than anything she wanted to toss her drink in his face.

"I'm glad you're here. Why don't we find a table and sit down? Catch up."

Phillip took a step closer, and she could smell his aftershave. Her stomach rolled at the scent and memories of their relationship sprang from their hiding places. She'd rather sit and visit with a rattlesnake than her ex. "I don't think so. We don't need to catch up." When she ended their relationship, she thought she'd made her feelings crystal clear.

Phillip ignored her words and reached for her hand. Ice-cold fear shot through her, and she glanced around for the Secret Service agents assigned to her. She'd asked them to hold back tonight. After all, everyone in the room had gone through security on their way in and the event was by invitation only.

"Let's put the past behind us, Sara. We're both here alone tonight." Ignoring her response, he pulled her toward him.

It's a room full of people, I'm safe. Sara tried to pull her arm away without making a scene. If she made a lot of commotion other people would notice. If possible she wanted to keep her run-in with Phillip under the radar.

"She's not alone."

Sara whipped her head around fast enough to give herself whiplash at the sound of Christopher's voice.

"Sorry I was gone so long. Congressman Roberts stopped me. You know how he can go on." Christopher took her free hand and pulled her possessively against his side. With no other choice, Phillip released her hand.

Sara felt Christopher drape his arm around her shoulder. The feel of his hand on her bare shoulder sent shivers of excitement down her arm, extinguishing the fear she'd felt moments earlier.

"Is there a problem here, Sara?" Although Christopher asked her the question, she noticed that he never looked away from Phillip.

"Phillip Young," Phillip said extending his hand. "We were just catching up. Sara and I are old friends."

Sara counted the seconds that passed as Phillip stood with his hand extended and Christopher made no move to accept it. She wanted to smile at the cut by Christopher. Phillip wasn't used to being ignored. He thought highly of himself and figured everyone else should too.

"It didn't look that way to me," Christopher said coldly.

When he looked over at her, Sara shook her head hoping he'd get the hint she wanted to drop the issue.

"Everything is fine. I was wondering where you were, but if Roberts got a hold of you that explains it." On impulse Sara dropped a brief kiss on Christopher's cheek hoping the tiny display of affection would add to the charade.

The second her lips left his cheek Christopher turned his head toward her, his chocolate brown eyes taking everything in.

"Aren't you going to introduce us?" Phillip asked letting his hand fall back to his side.

Phillip's voice pulled her attention away from Christopher. Before she answered she snaked her arm around his waist comforted by the feel of his body next to hers.

"Phillip, I'm sure you've heard of Christopher Hall of Hall Technology."

Sara forced herself to contain her smirk as the demeanor of the man before her changed. His eyes became the size of saucers, and he pulled his attention off her and turned it toward Christopher.

"Yes, I have. It's nice to meet you. I've heard great things about your company."

Sara half expected Phillip to fall to his knees and worship Christopher. It was all about money and power to him. All he cared about was who could help him get the most of both.

"Senator Healy wanted to see us before we leave, and I'm ready to go now." Christopher infused just the right amount of seduction in his tone.

"I better find him then. Goodnight Phillip."

She didn't wait for an answer. Instead she allowed Christopher to lead her toward the other end of the grand ballroom where tables had been set for dinner.

"Thank you." Sara stopped at an empty table in a far corner. "You arrived at just the right time."

Without saying a word, he pulled out a chair and gestured for her to sit. "Who was that anyway?"

"My ex. I don't know what he's doing here. I don't remember seeing him on the guest list." Sara heard the contempt in her voice but couldn't do anything about it. "Speaking of which, what are you doing here?" Now that a scene with Phillip had been avoided, it dawned on her that Christopher shouldn't be there either.

Christopher sat across the table from her and leaned back in his chair. He appeared to be a man without a care in the world and completely comfortable in her presence, despite the night they'd shared weeks ago.

The memory of waking up with his arm draped across her stomach filled her head. Over the past few weeks her memories of that night popped up time and time again, but only when she was alone. A fact she was grateful for. No such luck tonight. Warmth spread across her face and she hoped the lighting in the ballroom kept Christopher from seeing her blush.

"I've known David Healy for a few years. We belong to the same country club. We played golf right before Jake's wedding, and he invited me."

During their next meeting she would remind David to keep her apprised of who he issued invites to. As his chief of staff she needed to be in the loop on all things. Not to mention it would've been helpful to know Christopher was coming tonight.

"You did make it," Senator Healy said, approaching their table.

A man in his mid-forties, Senator Healy was the type who most would overlook in a crowd. A graduate of Columbia University, he'd built his entire life around one goal, making it to the United States Senate despite the fact he didn't have any family connections. She admired him for that. Accomplishing exactly what he'd achieved was her ultimate goal for the future.

The Senator pulled a chair out from the table and joined them. "And I see you've met my talented Chief of Staff. She came to work for me instead of the President himself," he said chuckling at his usual joke.

"We've known each other a long time. Christopher and my brother were roommates in college."

"I didn't realize there was a connection between you two," the Senator said pointing a finger back and forth between them. "So have you thought anymore about what we discussed?" Senator Healy asked before turning his attention to Sara. "I told him about the education initiative we want to get though."

Christopher nodded. "That's one of the reasons I am here tonight."

One of the reasons? What were his other reasons? She wanted to ask but knew it wasn't any of her business. Besides asking might give him the wrong impression.

"Excellent. That's what I wanted to hear," the senator said. "Sara, set up a meeting for us with Christopher." Pushing his chair back, he came to his feet. "I look forward to our meeting." The senator shook hands with Christopher before rejoining the guests in the ballroom.

Sara gripped her hands together, her nails digging into her skin. A meeting with her boss and her brother's best friend, with whom she'd had a one-night stand—could anything be more awkward? Doubtful, but stranger things happened.

"I'm staying in Providence for the weekend, so I'll call your assistant on Monday to arrange a meeting." If she avoided talking about anything personal tonight perhaps he would too.

"Call me directly. There's no need for you to go through Caroline." Christopher rested both elbows on the table and leaned closer.

Before she could stop herself, her eyes dropped to his large hands sprawled on the table and her skin tingled at the memory of them on her body. Immediately, her pulse quickened. "Okay," she said, sounding a little breathless.

"I thought I would spend a few days here myself. I haven't been on the East Coast in a while. What are your plans for tomorrow?"

She could lie. If she told him she had a previous engagement, he'd never know the difference. Sara opened her mouth, an excuse on the tip of her tongue, but the words wouldn't come. Although people in Washington were rumored to lie left and right to suit their own needs and agendas, she wasn't able to. Never had been in fact. For as long as she could remember her mom drilled into her that a true lady never lied. Omitting details was one thing, like not telling her brother about her one-night stand, but out and out lying just felt wrong. *A true lady doesn't have one-night stands either.*

"Nothing specific," the words slid from her mouth. She hadn't lied.

"How about dinner then? You can tell me more about this initiative David wants me to support."

Sara nodded in agreement. Perhaps working with Christopher would be the best way to get over her awkward feelings about Hawaii.

On the other side of the glass elevator, the city lights twinkled in the evening sky. Rolling her neck she tried to work out the tension that had settled there hours earlier. Normally these events gave her an adrenaline boost, but not tonight. While the evening had started out like any other, it had gone downhill fast, picking up speed along the way.

"What a night," she said to herself as the elevator reached her floor. The doors opened to a deserted hallway. She had the entire floor to herself, Secret Service made sure of that. Not that it would've been a problem, anyway considering the hotel belonged to Sherbrooke Enterprises.

Slipping her keycard into the lock, she pushed open the door, kicked off her Christian Louboutin heels, and headed straight for the bathroom with its oversized tub. She needed a long soak in the tub to wash away her stress. Her entire body felt tight as if it was about to snap, since she'd heard first Phillip's and then Christopher's voice. Not that she wasn't grateful for Christopher's interference. When he'd wrapped his arm around her waist anchoring her to his side, her fear disappeared.

Yet she'd hoped not to see Christopher for a very long time. Mortification, along with several other emotions, set in every time she thought of her behavior that night in Hawaii. If David had told her about his invitation to Christopher maybe she could have prepared herself for seeing him again.

To top off the weekend, now she was going to have dinner with him. Sara slid into the water, the heat immediately easing the tension in her body. Too bad it couldn't do the same for her warring emotions. Inhaling and exhaling slow measured breaths, Sara pushed Christopher from her mind. Tomorrow there would be enough time to deal with all her feelings he evoked. Tonight she needed to relax then get a good night's sleep.

With a hand towel, Christopher cleared the steam from the bathroom mirror. Then he reached for his contact lenses. Without those he ran the risk of slitting his own throat when he shaved the stubble that had grown since he shaved that morning. Two shaves in the same day wasn't his norm. When he could get away with it, he didn't even shave every day, but tonight there was no way around it.

Using his shaving brush, he covered his cheeks with a layer of shaving soap and reached for the straight edge razor he favored. While an electric razor would be quicker, he preferred the extra close shave the old-fashioned tool gave him. His sister, Caroline, loved to give him a hard time about the fact that his life revolved around the state-of-the-art in technology, yet he shaved with an instrument some men wouldn't even recognize.

As he scraped away the five o'clock shadow, his mind wandered to the evening ahead and a sharp pang of uneasiness pierced his gut. On so many levels taking Sara out tonight was wrong. Yeah, sure he'd asked her out, under the ruse that they could discuss the senator's new education plan while they ate, something that could wait until he met with them in Washington. The real reason he'd asked her was to spend time with her and get a sense of her feelings toward him. If that night in Hawaii hadn't happened, he'd never even entertain the idea that there might be something between them. Hawaii had happened, though, and he couldn't get it out of his mind. And he'd tried. Man, how he'd tried. He'd been out on dates with two different women since then, but neither had even remotely turned him on the way Sara had. On both occasions he'd dropped his date off at her place and had gone home alone.

After wiping any remaining shaving soap from his face, Christopher ran a hand through his damp hair, satisfied with the image looking back at him. It was an image that had taken years to develop. The self-assured man gazing back at him now hadn't always existed. In fact until college, he'd been the exact opposite, and he had his friendship with Jake to thank for much of that.

And how do I repay the guy? By sleeping with his sister. Even worse if the opportunity arose again, he didn't know if he'd be able to pass it up. Sara had intrigued him since the minute she walked into their dorm room freshman year. Back then she hadn't given the geeky nerd with the coke-bottle glasses a second look. Yet after her brother's wedding, she'd done so much more than that. Afterward she brushed it off as no big deal, yet he didn't completely believe her. Sure she showed up in magazine headlines from time to time with her name attached to a man, but nothing like her brother had before meeting Charlie.

Regardless of what type of life she led, she was supposed to be off-limits to him. You just didn't get involved with your friend's sister... period. Despite knowing this, he still planned to have dinner with her tonight. He just couldn't pass up the opportunity and if Jake found out he'd be able to say it'd been a business meeting.

"As long as I keep it out of the bedroom, it'll be okay," Christopher said to the image in the mirror as he buttoned his shirt. "How hard can that be?" Switching off the light he left, eager for the night ahead.

The candle in the center of the table flickered, casting Sara's face in a warm glow. What had he been thinking when he made these reservations? A private candle-lit room at Lucerne was not the place to bring a beautiful woman you had no business getting involved with. A better choice would've been a family friendly restaurant with bright lights and lots of loud music. *Too late now.*

They both remained silent while a waiter presented them with their drinks and promised to return when they had made their dinner choices. So far neither had spoken much beyond the general pleasantries.

"You said you wanted to know more about David's education plan," Sara said kicking off a real conversation.

He tried to maintain eye contact. No easy task tonight. A stray piece of her golden blonde hair had escaped her elegant updo, and it kept brushing against her collarbone. His fingers itched to brush the hair away and tuck it back behind her ear.

At the sound of her voice, Christopher's eyes flew away from the teasing strand and back to her face. "Yes. When we played golf he mentioned that he'd put together a new initiative merging technology and education and that it would soon come before the Senate for a vote."

"It's a multifaceted plan for improving public education by promoting science, engineering, and technology in our public schools in a variety of ways. First he wants to get the latest technology into schools at all grade levels, whether it's a small school in Greenwich, Connecticut or a large inner city school in Detroit. At the same time, raise the current standards used in schools."

The minute she'd mentioned the words education, science, and engineering his interest had been piqued. Yet the way her eyes literally came alive as she spoke and the excitement coming through her voice only pulled him in further. If it hadn't been for his love of science and computers, he'd be just another guy from Wisconsin.

Sara leaned forward in her excitement as she continued to tell him about the plan, giving him an excellent view of her cleavage. A fact she probably didn't realize and one he had no business noticing. Still he did. Any man in his position would.

Look away. Reaching for the menu he hadn't looked at, he opened it. He already knew what he wanted. The restaurant was one of his favorites in the city, but the inside of the menu gave him something other than Sara to study.

"Have you decided on what you're having?" Christopher asked when Sara paused in her explanation.

He almost sighed with relief when she leaned back in her chair and reached for her own untouched menu.

"No, not yet. Is there anything you recommend?"

"Everything is great, but they outdo themselves when it comes to seafood."

"Then I'll have to go with the shrimp scampi," she said just before the waiter returned.

Throughout dinner they discussed the new education plan. The more she told him about it, the more he felt it was something he could get behind and support. "When you get back to Washington let David know he has me on board." Christopher rested an elbow on the edge of the table.

A full true smile, not one of her society smiles, spread across Sara's face revealing a tiny dimple in her cheek. "Excellent. I think you'll be the perfect spokesperson for it."

He didn't know how much Sara knew about him, but nearly everyone in the world knew he'd come from an average background and turned himself into a technology billionaire.

"I'm surprised he didn't tag you for the role." With her excitement for the plan and her recognizable name, she'd make an excellent spokesperson.

Sara's smile disappeared. "He did but I refused. It would feel like I'm using the Sherbrooke name to get it passed. I plan to make my own way in DC without relying on my family name."

He understood her reasons, and admired her for her determination.

With the topic of the new bill exhausted for the time being, he turned his thoughts to other possible topics for conversation while they waited for dessert. "How did your mom handle the news when she learned about Jake's wedding?"

Sara's delicate shoulders rose and fell causing the stray piece of hair to sway back and forth, taunting him. "I haven't talked to him. But I don't think he has told her yet. If he has she hasn't called me. But he should tell her soon before the media gets wind of it." Sara paused as the waiter appeared with their desserts. "I don't envy him. I wouldn't want to tell her either," Sara said with no hint of humor in her voice.

He smiled despite the seriousness in her voice. "You and me both. I have to confess though, I would love to be a fly on the wall when he does tell her."

A sweet laugh escaped from Sara. "That would be entertaining," she said before turning her attention to the New York cheesecake before her.

Christopher focused on his own dessert. She hadn't spoken to Jake either.

Was she avoiding her brother as well or did they just not talk much? He thought Jake told him once that he and Sara were close.

"He hasn't said anything to you?" Sara asked, her face clouded with uneasiness.

"The last time he called, I was in a meeting." Although not a lie it wasn't the complete truth either. Jake had called him twice since the wedding. The first time he'd texted Jake back saying he was on his way to a meeting. He hadn't responded at all to the second call.

Sara nodded and he got the impression that she knew he was avoiding her brother. Probably because she was too.

Chapter 4

Less than a week later, Sara found herself once again seated across from Christopher. This time they weren't in a candle-lit restaurant, but rather in Senator Healy's office. As agreed, she had called Christopher directly after returning to Washington and set up a meeting with the senator in DC.

Now as the three of them sat there, Senator Healy explained the finer details of the education initiative he and Senator Kenny were pushing. Much to Christopher's credit, he asked insightful questions regarding how the new plan would be implemented and what kind of timetable would apply. Since he'd already told her he was on board, she guessed his questions had more to do with his genuine interest and not because he'd changed his mind.

"This is something I can support, so what exactly do you need me to do?" Christopher asked directing his question to both her and Senator Healy.

"Just what we wanted to hear, right Sara?" David didn't give her an opportunity to answer before launching into his next sentence. "Money is always a must for these types of things, and we need to get the word out. People need to know about the proposed initiative and how it will benefit their children and grandchildren. Once the public is behind it, the senators and representatives will be more likely to vote in favor of it. We'd like you to do a few TV ads to promote the plan. Who better than you to be the spokesperson for it?"

Sara felt Christopher's eyes on her and couldn't stop herself from looking in his direction. Somehow she resisted the urge to squirm in her chair as his brown eyes remained fixed on her. "Everyone knows your history. People will be more open to someone like you who has used education to change his life rather than a Hollywood celebrity." Prior to the meeting, she and David had discussed how best to sell their plan.

Christopher nodded once, his eyes never leaving her face. "You're probably right. But I think it'd be even more powerful if you did the ads with me. From a marketing point of view an ad with me and the President's daughter is ideal."

"I agree, but Sara refuses to attach her name publicly to the plan."

"She told me that, but maybe she'll reconsider." Christopher looked directly at her. "What do you say Sara? Will you work on this with me? These ads will attach both our names to the plan. And you know the importance of this initiative. It's not like we're talking about some fluff piece of legislation. If this passes it would improve education for millions of children."

This time she did squirm in her seat as a lead ball plummeted through her stomach not only at the thought of working with Christopher but at putting aside a personal rule she'd made when she joined David's staff. How could she work with someone she felt so uncomfortable around? Sure she respected the man. It'd be hard not to considering all he'd achieved. Plus he'd never once run to the paparazzi with a story about her family or her brother despite his connection, something a lesser man would've done without any hesitation. That didn't change what had happened between them.

He's not Phillip. She let her gaze trail over Christopher while his full attention was once again on the senator. The man across the table looked nothing like the man who'd tried to ruin her father's political career.

Memories of Christopher intervening when Phillip stopped her at the fundraiser came rushing back to her. If it hadn't been for him that night, there definitely would've been a scene. Phillip just couldn't take no for an answer.

"I agree with you Christopher, but she's been adamant about this one." David's statement forced her to store away her thoughts of Christopher for the moment and concentrated on what he said. He was right. This education initiative would affect millions if it passed. And with Christopher on board too, it would no longer be just her name, attached which made her feel a little better about publicly endorsing it. But working with a man who she'd slept with seemed like a disaster waiting to happen. Why couldn't Christopher stick with her original plan?

Beneath the solid cherry conference table, Sara tapped a foot against the floor, the sound muffled by the thick rug as she made her decision. "If you both think it's necessary, the two of us can do it." The words flowed from her mouth before she stopped to consider her exact word choice. Once the words escaped, Sara looked over at Christopher. There was no mistaking the heated gaze he threw her way before glancing down at his watch. A hot flush burned her face and she jotted down some notes on her legal pad to keep from looking at either man.

David slapped his hand on the table. Instantly, Sara jerked her head up.

"Excellent. I have contacts in Hollywood who are all set to start filming the commercial for us. They just need my final okay and you two."

An argument against the new plan sat on the tip of her tongue, yet she couldn't get the words through her lips. Despite her uneasiness at working with Christopher and attaching her name to the initiative, she had to admit it was a good idea. If they showed their support together it would make a more powerful selling tool.

Out of the corner of her eye, she watched Christopher wrap his hands around a glass of water and raise it to his lips. He had such large hands, yet their night together they had been so gentle and smooth. No rough skin or calluses ruined his hands. Even from across the table she could see how short and clean he kept his nails. There were no ragged edges or torn skin. For half a second she closed her eyes almost able to feel his hands sliding down her back and up her legs again.

"If your people are ready for us, Sara and I can fly back to California together in a few days."

The momentary daydream went up in a puff of smoke when Christopher spoke.

"I think that can be arranged," David said before turning toward Sara. "Call Bruce Gordon, tell him everyone is on board and that we want to get started ASAP."

Sara nodded. "Won't they need time to write scripts?" She backed the senators' proposed bill one hundred percent, but she wanted this done right. Ad campaigns took time and required the correct amount of preparation.

"Already prepared. I made a calculated guess that Christopher would agree. Before filming you can go over the scripts and adjust them as you see necessary," David answered, his usual confidence leaking into his words.

David's words didn't surprise her. If the senator had any characteristic in overabundance, it was confidence. Hence he always assumed people would fall in line with his plans. While she sometimes found it annoying, he wasn't the only politician to suffer that flaw. Even her father fell into that category from time to time. Sara shot a glance toward Christopher. Going by his expression, the senator's assumption didn't shock him either.

"If we're through here, I'll contact Bruce." Sara uncrossed her legs and stood.

"We are for now," David said.

After gathering up her notes, Sara left both men seated in the senator's office and returned to her office with a list of tasks.

৩৩৩৩

Dark blue suit, check. Lilac dress, check. Sara went down the list crossing each item off as she added it to her suitcase. Since the year she first left for boarding school, she always made a list of the items she wanted to pack regardless of whether she was going away for two nights or for two months. Some might consider the habit ridiculous especially since she could buy what she forgot, but she couldn't shake the habit.

Once she reached the bottom of her list, Sara closed the suitcase and slipped it off the bed. Then she turned her attention to her monthly calendar. The day before she had spent over an hour rearranging meetings so she could make this impromptu trip to California. While she thought she'd managed to reschedule everything, she figured one last pass over things wouldn't hurt.

Halfway through the first week, a popular heavy metal song her brother liked came from her phone. *Jake.* For a few heartbeats, Sara sat frozen, her hand poised above the phone. She still hadn't talked to him since Hawaii. Rarely did she go this long without at least a quick phone call to say hi and she found she missed talking to him. Before she could change her mind, Sara picked up the phone. "Hello."

"Are you in DC this week?" Jake asked after greeting her. "Or was this the week of the fundraiser in Providence?"

"The fundraiser was last week." Sara drew rows of connecting triangles along the edge of a piece of paper.

"Good. Why don't you come spend the weekend? Charlie has the weekend off and Mom and Dad are coming for dinner on Saturday."

Sara's ears perked up at the mention of her parents. She knew her brother still hadn't told them about his marriage. If he had, their mom would've called her by now. "Need reinforcements big brother?" She couldn't stop herself from teasing him. He did the same thing every chance he got.

"If I did, I'd call Dylan. If anyone can unruffled Mom's feathers it's him," Jake answered with amusement. "I just thought I'd get you out of your little office on the Hill before you turn into a workaholic like our brother."

Turning the paper she began another group of triangles. "I'd love to see the fireworks when you drop the news, but I'm leaving for California tomorrow. The senator asked us to do some ads supporting his new education initiative." Only after she spoke the words did she realize that she'd used us rather than me.

"Us? Who's us?" Jake asked, genuine curiosity in his voice.

Damn Jake for being so attentive. While working with Christopher was no big deal, she hated the idea of bringing him up with her brother. It only reminded her further of the friendship she'd put at risk. "David got Christopher on board. He thought an ad featuring the two of us would boost support with the public more than an ad featuring only him."

"Doesn't surprise me that he signed on. When you see him tell him my number hasn't changed. I've called him a few times and he hasn't called back."

Sara loaned her head back against her chair, her eyes closed. "I'll tell him."

"I can think of someone else who would support this legislation if you asked her," Jake said, his voice taking a serious tone.

She knew without him continuing whom he had in mind. As an elementary school teacher Callie had a passion for education. And it wasn't that she hadn't considered it already.

"Callie would be a great person to have on board with her background, and you know how much the American public loves her."

Everything Jake said was true and the very reason she'd already considered her half-sister. Still Sara held back from calling her. While their relationship was more cordial now than when they first met they were far from best buds. She'd created the situation herself and she'd undo it if she could. Just thinking about the way she treated Callie made her cringe.

Images of the conversation she had when Callie first entered their lives, played across her mind like a bad movie. Hoping to get rid of the images, Sara opened her eyes and stared up at the ceiling. "I'll consider it, Jake. You know it's complicated."

On the other end of the line Jake remained silent and she guessed her brother was formulating his rebuttal.

"Only you can fix that."

Perhaps her brother was correct, but that didn't mean she wanted to reopen any old wounds. Right now she and Callie were able to be in the same room together and be civil to each other. If Sara reminded Callie of her previous behavior, who knew what might happen?

"Like I said Jake, I'll think about it." For now it was all she could say.

"Whatever. Call me when you get back to DC."

She knew her brother well enough to know it was taking most of his self-control to keep himself from pressing the issue further. "I will. Good luck with Mom and Dad."

Sara hit end on the phone after saying goodbye, her entire body a jumble of emotions. Although she hadn't lied to Jake, hiding what had happened with Christopher felt like a betrayal. To top that off, her shame regarding Callie had her stomach in knots. If Callie had only showed up a year earlier or any time before she met Phillip for that matter, maybe their relationship would've been different. Before Phillip entered her life, she'd been more trusting and more open to starting new relationships. Her time with Phillip managed to kill all that. Now she approached all new relationships, regardless of the person, with apprehension and suspicion. In fact, since Phillip she hadn't developed any new friendship or let anyone get close to her— at least not until her brother's wedding. Something about Christopher allowed her to drop her guard. While she attributed some of it to the cosmos she'd consumed, that didn't completely account for that night. The suspicion that usually shadowed all her new acquaintances never appeared that night. The only emotions she felt that evening were attraction and curiosity.

Now that she'd let him get close, he often popped into her thoughts. He didn't belong there, she knew that. Yet he kept making an appearance and now she had a whole week ahead of her with him around. Somehow she needed to push thoughts of their night together aside and focus on the task at hand. Exactly how though she hadn't figured out yet.

"But I will," she muttered as she turned her attention back to her calendar.

☙❧☙❧

Sara struggled to stifle a yawn the next morning as the limo stopped at Reagan International Airport. The previous evening she'd gotten little sleep. After talking to Jake she'd finished packing and crawled into bed around one o'clock. Unfortunately, sleep had eluded her. Instead her conversation with Jake and uneasiness about this trip with Christopher weighed heavily on her mind. Now, however, the sleep she'd craved so much the night before threatened to overtake her.

"Another late night working, Ms. Sherbrooke?" Colin, one of the Secret Service agents assigned to her detail, asked from the seat across from her in the limo.

"I had a lot of loose ends to take care of before this trip. And please Colin, call me Sara." She'd been telling the agent that ever since he became part of her security detail, but so far he continued to address her as Ms. Sherbrooke.

Colin nodded slightly. "I'll try to remember that ma'am."

Sara fought the urge to roll her eyes. Ma'am was worse than Ms. Sherbrooke. Oh how she wished Raymond, the Secret Service agent Colin replaced, would come back.

"Andrea and I reviewed your proposed itinerary while in California. We have a few issues we want to review with you."

Tossing her phone into her Coach purse, Sara slipped the straps onto her shoulder and reached for the leather briefcase at her feet. "Let's plan on doing it once we get to the hotel."

She didn't want to do it all. She knew the agents were only doing their job, but sometimes she found their presence intrusive. In fact she envied Jake for telling them to take a hike. But as much as she didn't care for their constant presence, she did feel safer with them around.

The door to the limo opened allowing a blast of unusually cool air into the vehicle. "That should be fine," Colin replied before exiting the limo first.

Before following the agent, Sara slipped on the jacket that matched her red skirt, grateful for the protection it gave her against the cool early morning air.

At least it'll be warm in California. Smoothing out any wrinkles, Sara made her way to the stairs leading up to Christopher's Gulf Stream jet. With her right foot poised over the bottom step, she stopped. It had made sense to fly back with him, despite the fact that she could use the family jet or one from the senatorial pool. They could use the flight time to review the scripts, which had been emailed to her. She stood there, though her body tensed and her mind telling her to turn around and scrap the whole trip.

Everything will be fine. The sound of her heel hitting the metal step vibrated through her entire body and she forced her left foot onto the first step too.

"Perfect timing. Did your driver already get your bags?" Christopher appeared at the plane door.

That morning he'd gone for what she called the super-casual look. With his faded jeans, plain gray T-shirt and sneakers he reminded her a little more of the guy who'd roomed with her brother instead of the ultra-wealthy CEO the rest of the world knew.

"All set." Sara forced herself to smile despite the tightness in her chest. She couldn't explain it, but she felt as if each step up the stairs was taking her further away from her life as she knew it and closer to something else. Something new and unexpected.

Christopher took a step back so she could enter the plane. "Excellent. As soon as you're settled we can go."

Forty minutes into the flight, Sara ditched her jacket and reached for her cup of tea. Both she and Christopher had finished their breakfast and had gone straight to work. Or at least she tried to work. Her brain had other ideas. It wanted to focus on the man seated across from her. Once again Sara's eyes traveled back to Christopher, the man who visited her dreams every night. The man, who despite knowing it was a huge mistake, she wanted to get to know better.

Despite her inability to work, Christopher didn't suffer from the same fate. Since opening his laptop, he hadn't looked up once. A fact that actually annoyed her a little. Having a man ignore her wasn't something that ever happened.

Perhaps sensing her gaze, Christopher looked up, his warm chocolate brown eyes locking on her face. Heat instantly scorched her cheeks. It was one thing to study someone but another to be caught doing it.

"Sorry, I haven't been very good company," he said, his eyes never leaving her face. "I'm almost done with this."

The soft leather felt cool against the back of her thighs as she shifted in her seat, causing her skirt to ride up her thigh. "Don't worry, I'm fine."

Christopher's eyes dropped down to the screen once again. She heard his fingers moving over the keyboard then he closed the laptop and his gaze once again settled on her face.

"All done. I'm all yours." His mouth curved into a wide smile.

Memories of their one night together exploded in her mind. They hadn't spoken of it on the three occasions they'd seen each other yet she couldn't help but wonder if he ever thought about it. *Too bad asking is out of the question.*

"You should be careful who you say that to." She hoped a little teasing would help her think of him as a brother type rather than a lover. After all she joked with Jake all the time. "Say that to the wrong woman and you'll find yourself holding a pumice stone giving a pedicure."

Without warning he leaned forward and lifted her leg toward him. The feel of his hand on her bare calf sent shivers through her body.

"Since it looks like you had one recently, I guess I'm safe." He lifted his head from his inspection of her coral pink toenails. Slowly he put her foot back down to the floor and released it. But even after he moved his hand away she could feel it on her skin.

Why did I do that? Christopher gripped his armrest, hard enough to make his knuckles turn white to prevent himself from touching her again. "So how did you end up working for Senator Healy? Didn't he run against your father's friend George Beck in the primary?" A discussion of politics should be a good way to keep them both distracted.

"My father wanted me to work with George. Actually he guaranteed me a spot on his staff if I wanted it."

"Then why did you go with Healy? A lot of people didn't think he could win." Sara struck him as the type to follow the expectations of her family. Jake was the rebel, not Sara.

Sara shrugged one shoulder. "I like George. I've known him all my life, but I don't agree with his policies. A lot of them are too old-fashioned. Besides, I wanted to earn my position, not have it given to me."

Prior to a few weeks ago, he'd thought of Sara as little more than a spoiled rich girl. Sure he knew she was well-educated, but he hadn't realized she used her education or had any aspirations for the future. Obviously he couldn't have been more wrong. Not only did she have aspirations, she wanted to achieve them through hard work like everyone else.

"Makes sense. But why Healy? I'm sure half a dozen senators or congressmen would love to have you on their team." Having the daughter of a popular president in your corner had to be a plus in politics not to mention she had a law degree from Harvard University.

"I liked his platform. It was something I could rally behind. Take this legislation of his for education. He understands the importance of boosting the sciences and technology in schools. Many of the senior politicians are stuck in the past and don't see that our schools are lagging behind in those areas." As she spoke more emotion poured into her voice.

Christopher raised both hands in surrender. "You don't have to convince me. I agree, remember," he said with a laugh.

"Sorry," she said looking a bit sheepish, "this topic gets me a little emotional."

Christopher dropped his hands. "I never would've guessed."

"I think we have a good chance of getting it approved. When these ads run, I think people will realize how much the country will benefit and contact their senators urging them to vote for the bill. Senator Healy was right. You are the perfect spokesperson. Although I'm not sure he needs me too." Sara reached for her teacup as she spoke.

"You're wrong there. Trust me on this one." Christopher emptied his coffee cup and asked the flight attendant for more.

"Are those the proposed scripts?" He glanced over at the papers in front of Sara. She'd been folding and unfolding the corners of the pages through the majority of their conversation.

Sara looked down and he got the impression she'd forgotten about the papers. "Yes. They were emailed to me late last night. For the most part they're good, but I thought we might want to tweak a few lines."

"We have time now. Why don't we go over them?" Christopher said coming to his feet. Before Sara could agree or disagree he moved to the other side of the table and sat down next to her. "May I?" He leaned closer and reached for the papers. As he did he caught the slightest smell of her perfume. A light flowery fragrance, it was the same one she'd worn in Hawaii and at the fundraiser. Normally, he didn't remember the smell of a particular perfume. Having grown up in a house with four sisters he had constantly been around it, but he couldn't tell you which sister favored what fragrance. Somehow though he knew the one Sara wore now was the same one from those other nights.

Sara released the papers. "I marked the sentences that I think need work."

It didn't take long for him to read over the material and commit it to memory. Just one of the benefits of a photographic memory, and he had never been more grateful for it than he was now. Sitting so close to Sara with her perfume teasing his nose destroyed most of his concentration.

Christopher shifted in his seat in an attempt to put more space between them. "I agree this sentence needs work." He pointed at a sentence underlined in red. "Do you have any ideas?"

Sara reached for the papers and her hand brushed against his. "I wrote some ideas on the back."

He looked up and his eyes immediately zeroed in on her lips. The memory of how perfect they felt against his made his body ache to hold her close and taste her again. How would she respond if he kissed her now? Would she push him away or wrap her arms around him?

"How do they sound?"

Her question intruded on his thoughts. He hadn't heard a word she'd read. "Sounds good." He dropped his eyes back down to the papers. If he stopped staring at her mouth maybe he'd get some work done. "This line here, I like already." He pointed to the next underlined sentence on the page. "But let's work on this last one here."

ᘓᕲᘓᕲᘓᕲ

The sound of wheels hitting the ground jolted him awake. Stretching both arms over his head he tried to work the stiffness out of his shoulders and neck. *How long have I been out?* Christopher glanced across the plane expecting to see Sara sleeping as well. Throughout their time working on the script, she kept yawning. Instead he found her sitting, her body rigid, gripping the armrests of her seat.

"Hey are you okay?" he asked, getting out of his seat and moving toward her.

"I dread the landings," she admitted. "I'm not a big fan of flying in general, but I really hate the landings."

He opened his mouth to speak but then closed it. Since he knew she traveled a lot he couldn't imagine her being afraid of flying.

"I know. More people die in car accidents than plane crashes, but I still don't like it." She released the death grip she had on the seat. "And I've done it so much you'd think it wouldn't bother me anymore, but it does."

Obviously, she'd had this conversation before. "At least you don't let your fear stop you." So many people refused to try things because of their fears. The fact that she didn't let her fear interfere with her life, told him a great deal about her.

"Not when it comes to flying anyway."

Her comment made him wonder what other things she feared. It certainly sounded as if she had others, although he couldn't picture her fearing much. She, like everyone else in her family, came across confident and sure of their place in the world. Not the type of person who shied away from things because they were scared.

Maybe she's afraid of snakes. His mom and sisters were petrified of snakes. They wouldn't even look at the snakes behind glass. "Sorry, I fell asleep. I didn't intend to."

Sara unfastened her seat belt. "It's okay. I read a book. I started it a month ago and still haven't finished it. Just don't have enough time."

What type of books did she enjoy? Did she lose herself in mysteries like his sister Caroline? Or did she prefer romances like his mom and sister Rachel? He didn't see her enjoying a horror. Then again over the past month he was learning that his previous view of her was far from accurate.

"A few extra hours in a day would come in handy some time." During the week he routinely worked eighteen-hour days but on the weekends, he left work behind whenever he could. Since he owned the company, he could do that. Sara didn't have that luxury, her schedule revolved around the senator's.

Gradually, the plane rolled to a complete stop and the flight attendant opened the door. Outside the window Christopher saw the limo he'd arranged to pick them up. Despite the fact that they'd been on the plane for hours, he didn't feel any immediate desire to rush off. During the flight their conversations covered several topics and he found he liked talking to her. He didn't do that with many women. Sure he talked to other women, but not usually about anything of consequence unless they were family members. Since becoming friends with Jake and then later making his first million, women tended to throw themselves at him but none really provided an intelligent conversation.

In the beginning they hoped to get to Jake through an association with him. Later they started to come because of his new wealth. Sara didn't need either and unlike many of the women who chased him she had a brain. He could carry on an intelligent conversation with her and use words with more than one syllable.

"Our meeting with Bruce Gordon is scheduled for ten o'clock tomorrow. You look tired. You should take the rest of the day off and relax," Christopher said, standing up. Without a second thought he reached for her leather briefcase on the floor by her feet. He couldn't stop himself from letting the back of his hand skim across her bare calf as he picked it up. Her bare legs had been taunting him ever since she'd stepped on board. His body started to respond at the touch. How could such a simple touch affect him so much? He barely touched her, yet his heart lurched with excitement and his pulse pounded.

"Are you ready to go?" He looked at her as he straightened up, prepared to tell her he'd carry her briefcase for her, yet the look on her face stopped him. A pale pink covered her cheeks. Her slate gray eyes were filled with desire and focused on his mouth.

Gratitude surged through him. It felt good to know the attraction he felt wasn't one-sided. Without stopping to think he bent toward her, intent on kissing her lush pink mouth. Halfway to his destination he stopped himself. Once already he crossed the line with Sara. Doing so again wasn't a wise idea. So instead of kissing her, he held out his hand to help her up.

During the ride from the airport to Sara's hotel both remained silent. While he didn't know what thoughts kept Sara quiet, he knew what bothered him. How was he going to maintain a professional relationship with her as they worked? Just being around her in Washington and then again today on the plane, his thoughts had continuously returned to their night together. Each time they'd gotten together since then he'd wanted to repeat that night. He'd managed to hold himself back so far. Could he continue to do that as they worked closely together though? Not that he had much of a choice in the matter. Sara sat across from him facing the window. He'd seen the desire in her eyes when he touched her, was it possible she wanted to pick things up from Hawaii as much as he did?

The limo turned onto Santa Monica Boulevard and came to a stop in front of the Sherbrooke Plaza Hotel. Sara turned away from the window and looked at him. "After I email the script changes to Senator Healy the first thing I am going to do is sit in the hot tub."

The mental image her words created almost caused him to groan out loud. With the state his mind was already in, he didn't need an image of her soaking in a hot tub floating around. "I'll leave you to it." Rather than a hot tub, he needed a vat of ice. As soon as he got to his apartment he planned to take an ice cold shower. "I thought we could have dinner together tonight. If you're too tired we can skip it."

"After some time in the hot tub and some tea, I'll be fine. Dinner sounds lovely." She gifted him with one of her real smiles and he forgot how to breathe for half a second.

"Then I'll be by around six." Without waiting for a reply he slipped out of the car and extended a hand to help her out once again, thankful for all the proper etiquette instructions Jake had given him years earlier. One slender leg peeked out of the door, immediately catching his attention. When Sara's other foot touched the pavement his eyes made a trail from the coral nails poking out of her open-toed heels to the bare thighs her skirt revealed.

It's going to be a long night.

"You're not staying here?" Sara asked as she adjusted her skirt so that the hemline once again brushed her knees.

"I have a place in Los Angeles." He expected her to question him further but instead she took a step away.

"I'll see you tonight."

He stood next to the open car door and watched her walk away. Her strides were fluid and graceful as her long slender legs carried her toward the door. A quick glance around told him he wasn't the only male present who watched her either. When she disappeared into the hotel, Christopher climbed back into the limo. Yep, the next few days were going to be hell.

Chapter 5

Like many great plans, hers sounded perfect in her mind but the execution of it proved difficult. After checking into her room, she sent the suggested script changes she and Christopher made the senator and Bruce Gordon. Unfortunately, that was as far as she got in her grand plan. Before she could even change out of the clothes she'd traveled in, the Secret Service agents responsible for her security detail insisted she sit down with them and review her schedule for the next several days—a task that took much longer than necessary. In all honesty, she thought the agents over-planned by insisting that they cover every possible contingency no matter how improbable. She always kept her views to herself though. They were doing their jobs. So she always handled their presence and views with a proverbial smile.

By the time they finished there hadn't been enough time for a relaxing soak so she had to settle for a shower. Somehow she managed it in record time and ten minutes later she stood in front of the closet studying her clothes.

Would Christopher mind if they stayed in and ordered room service? She could call and ask him. If she called he might assume she needed an early night and suggest they not get together at all. As tired as she was, she didn't want to spend the entire night alone in her hotel room watching television. She wanted company. Okay maybe she didn't want just anyone's company. She wanted Christopher's. She enjoyed their conversation over dinner in Washington and today on the plane. He didn't speak to her as if she was some ditzy blonde like many men did or flatter her the entire time with some secret agenda in mind. Over the years both types of conversations had become almost the norm for her, even with some of the people on the Hill. Christopher, though, asked her insightful questions and challenged her views. He even managed to make her laugh, something she rarely did anymore. At the same time he always offered information about himself. During their last few conversations in fact she'd learned more about him than she'd learned in all the years he and her brother had been friends. And he didn't just share the information one could read online either.

Selecting a pair of designer skinny jeans and a pastel pink top, Sara carried them both back to the bed. If Christopher insisted they go out instead she could change. For now she planned on staying in for the evening. Pulling the top over her head, she buttoned the two buttons near the neck and then slipped the jeans on. After pulling her hair back in a ponytail, she sat down at the desk to tackle some work. If she kept up as much as possible while in California, when she returned to DC there wouldn't be piles of work waiting for her.

Less than half an hour later a knock at her hotel suite door pulled her attention away from her emails. She'd only been away from the office since the morning yet her in box was full. Closing the browser window, she came to her feet. Knowing that Secret Service would have only let Christopher up, she pulled open the door without asking who it was.

"I mentioned dinner right?" Christopher asked closing the door behind him. Dressed in a dark blue suit he looked like he'd just stepped off the cover of GQ magazine. "Or do you need more time to get ready? I can change our reservation time."

"You did. I thought we could stay in and get something sent up." After telling him her hopes for the evening she realized how they may sound to Christopher. While she meant them in a purely innocent way, he might think she wanted something more than just dinner. Especially considering their night together in Hawaii.

Sara moved to stand next to the table. "I'm a little tired and would rather stay in. Maybe get a movie," she said in an attempt to clarify her intentions for the evening. "If you really want to go out, we can. It'll only take me a few minutes to change."

Christopher reached for the knot in his red tie. "We can stay in." He slid the tie off his neck "I'd prefer that. I just assumed you'd want to go out." After taking off his jacket, he draped it and his tie over the back of a chair. Then he pulled his phone out and canceled their dinner reservations.

Pleased that he'd agreed, Sara found the room service menu. Like most five-star resorts, the room service menu was extensive and it didn't take either of them long to decide on a meal. While they waited for dinner Sara selected a bottle of wine from the suite's kitchenette. The day before she called the hotel manager and arranged to have the kitchenette stocked with beverages as well as fresh fruit and bagels. Then she grabbed the bowl of grapes from the refrigerator and carried everything back into the suite's sitting area where Christopher waited.

Now that his jacket and tie were gone, and he unbuttoned the top two buttons on his shirt, he looked much more relaxed but just as handsome. She liked seeing him like this. He seemed more like the person she remembered meeting when he'd roomed with Jake and a bit less like the man featured on the cover of business magazines.

"I hope you really don't mind that we stayed in tonight." Sara placed everything on the table, then poured them each a glass of wine.

"No complaints here."

He smiled as he accepted the glass of wine from her and for a moment she felt more like a twelve-year-old girl meeting one of her older brother's friends than a mature woman. "Do you live in LA?" She asked the first question that came to mind. She remembered he said he was staying at his apartment in the city.

"No. I purchased the apartment in LA for my parents to use when they come out to visit one of my sisters. She's a junior at UCLA. They refused to let me buy it for them, so I own it and they can use it whenever they want."

His answer caught her attention. He talked a little about his family on the plane, but she never read about them in any of the articles she'd seen. "How many sisters do you have?" Sara scooted back into the corner of the sofa and drew her knees up to her chest.

"Four sisters and they are all younger," he answered trying to sound as if it was a huge burden but the smile on his face ruined the effect. "Caroline works for me. Rachel and her husband still live in Wisconsin and have a two-year-old son. Laura is a junior at UCLA and Kristin will graduate from high school this June."

She never would've guessed he came from such a big family. "Lucky you. I'd trade a brother for a sister for a few days. Having two older ones isn't always a breeze." Overall Dylan and Jake were great and she couldn't deny she and Jake were especially close. However, both men could be overbearing from time to time, especially when she'd been growing up.

"Don't tell either of them I said this. I love them both but they drive me nuts sometimes. I always wanted a sister growing up."

Christopher laughed a deep rich sound. "I guess we all want what we don't have. I wanted a brother. I had a cousin I was close to as a kid, but it wasn't the same. At least you have one now. Are you two close?"

Sara pressed her lips together in an effort not to frown. "Not really," she admitted her voice low.

Sara didn't miss the questioning look he gave her. "Maybe that'll change. You only met, what two years ago?"

Before she thought better of it, Sara shook her head. "We didn't get off to a great start." Other than Jake no one else knew how much she regretted the way things started with Callie. "I didn't trust her after we all found out and I let her know it."

Sara searched his face for any sign of his thoughts regarding her confession. Most wouldn't understand or would think less of her. Christopher's expression reflected only a willingness to listen. Something only a handful of people offered her.

"Right before the family learned about Callie I had ended a year-long relationship with Phillip." She needed him to understand her state of mind at the time. "I let my feelings toward him control the way I treated her."

"That jerk from the fundraiser?"

Sara nodded yes as Beethoven's Fur Elise erupted from her phone and there was a knock at the door.

"Room service," a voice called out from the other side of the door.

Without waiting for Sara to react, Christopher rose. From her spot on the sofa she watched him cross the room, and she couldn't help but admire his retreating form. Just what did he look like without clothes? On their one night together the room had been dark and it was difficult to see. The next morning when they'd woken up he'd remained in bed until she left the room. Just by studying the way his clothes fit his body and the way he carried himself, she knew he put her last boyfriend to shame. Although a little taller than her brother Jake's six foot one, he appeared to be just as muscular. In her mind a picture formed of how she thought he looked. Closing her eyes she focused on it for a moment before picking up her phone and hitting ignore. Her mom could leave her a voice mail.

Her parents' dinner with Jake and Charlie had been tonight. More than likely her mom's call pertained to her brother's impromptu wedding weeks before. Or more specifically, why she hadn't told her mom about it. Not that she hadn't felt guilty about not telling her parents, but it wasn't her place. Instead she'd avoided both her parents as much as possible the last few weeks.

"I'm guessing that wasn't someone you wanted to talk to." Christopher removed the covered plates from the room-service cart.

Sara's stomach growled at the smells drifting from the plates and with a self-conscious laugh, she joined him at the table. "My mom. Jake invited them over for dinner tonight. He planned to tell them he and Charlie got married."

"Now that's a conversation I'd love to hear."

Sara grinned at Christopher's playful tone. "You and me both. I can't think of any way you could get me to change places with him though."

Their conversation over dinner covered everything from Elizabeth Sherbrooke's reaction to Jake's news to the commercials they were filming. Never once during their meal did they lapse into silence. Christopher found it refreshing. Rarely did he find a woman he could just talk to. Most didn't share the same interests and values or simply weren't interested in him. Rather they saw him as a big fat dollar symbol that could somehow enhance their lives.

A few weeks ago he wouldn't have thought he had anything in common with Sara Sherbrooke. Yet the more time he spent with her, the more he realized he'd been wrong. When she spoke of her family, and especially her regrets with her relationship to Callie, he knew family meant a lot to her. The fact that she'd refused a position with a highly respected senator told him she didn't depend on her family name to achieve her goals in life. But despite what he'd learned so far he found himself wanting to know even more. Although he shouldn't consider it, he wanted to dig down even further and get to know her on every level possible. Never before had he met a woman who he wanted to know like that.

Don't do anything you'll regret later. The warning rang in his head as he refilled Sara's wine glass. He had already taken a step down that path once and while his body wanted to repeat it, his logical brain couldn't decide if it was worth the risk.

"Do you think Jake survived dinner with your parents?" He could picture the way that dinner party and conversation must have played out.

Sara reached to adjust her hair and his eyes followed her every movement. Tonight she had her long blonde hair pulled up in a simple ponytail. Something he'd never seen on her and his fingers itched to pull it down. Her choice of hairstyles wasn't the only thing different about her tonight. He couldn't recall ever seeing her dress so casually, and he found it a definite turn on.

"You could always call him and find out," Sara answered.

He shifted his gaze toward the blank flat-screen TV on the wall. "Maybe I'll do that. Are you interested in a movie?" One of these days soon, he had to return Jake's call. They'd been friends too long not to.

"The hotel probably doesn't have many choices but what kind did you have in mind?"

Christopher looked back in Sara's direction just in time to see her run her tongue across her bottom lip licking off a droplet of wine. *A few hours in bed with you*. A mental image of them together sprang to life. "Anything but a romantic comedy," he answered grateful she couldn't read his thoughts. "And with this we can access my movie collection at home." He held up a small device no larger than a thumb drive attached to his key ring.

Sara stuck out her bottom lip in and over exaggerated pout. "What do you men have against romantic comedies? Have you ever seen one?"

She sounded like his sisters. Women in general just didn't get it. Unless a movie had a lot of action or spectacular special effects men didn't want to know anything about it. "They're chick movies. I'd rather sit through the ballet than watch one again." From across the table she glared at him. "Before you ask again, yes, I've seen them before. Four sisters, remember?"

Sara continued to glare at him. He thought she looked ridiculously cute doing it. Biting down on the inside of his cheek, he waited for her response.

"Fine, but I'm not watching some crazy superhero movie either."

He should've seen that one coming. Standing he plugged the device into the back of the mounted flat-screen television. Switching on the television with the remote, he pulled his cell phone from his pocket and connected to his personal movie collection. Immediately several movie categories came up on the screen. "How do you feel about the classics?" Before she answered he opened the category file so she could see what titles he owned.

"I've never seen anything like that before. Where did you get it?"

"It's not available yet. This is a working prototype I developed since I travel so much," he answered. "So do you see anything you like?" With his phone he scrolled down the list.

"Casablanca," Sara said, when the title popped up in the list.

She'd get no complaints from him. It was the first Bogart film he ever saw. And it had started his love of movies from Hollywood's early days. "Great choice." He selected the movie. "It's one of my favorite Bogart films."

Sara made herself comfortable on the long sofa. "Really? I like it, but I think my favorite is The Big Sleep with Lauren Bacall."

He never would've pegged her as a lover of classic movies. He assumed she enjoyed the latest releases more like his sisters. The only other person he knew that enjoyed the classics was his youngest sister Kristen but only original Alfred Hitchcock movies.

"I'd say that's in my top three followed by The Maltese Falcon."

"Then we can watch it tomorrow night if you have it," she said turning her face directly toward him.

For a moment he got lost in the depth of her gray eyes. Like everything else about her, they were beautiful and framed by incredibly long blonde eyelashes. Unable to blink or look away he held her gaze, glad that she couldn't see what was going through his mind.

"Sounds like a plan. I have all of Bogart's movies." The opening theme of the movie began, and he pulled his eyes away from Sara.

Somewhere around the middle of the film Christopher opened another bottle of wine. When he returned rather than sit back down in the chair, he sat down next to Sara on the sofa. When his leg came in contact with hers she sent him a questioning look but she didn't make any attempt to put space between them. Soon he found himself paying more attention to Sara than the movie. Every time she raised her glass to her lips or shifted her position, he knew it. Every nerve ending in his body sensed her presence. His skin screamed for the feel of her hands on his body.

Clenching his hands into tight fists, he mentally cursed himself for sitting so close. By doing so he was only punishing himself. Next to him Sara leaned toward him, her perfume teasing his overloaded senses even further.

"I know why Rick did it, but I always thought he shouldn't have let her go. It's obvious they love each other."

He saw her lips moving and knew she had said something. His mind didn't register the words though. It stayed focused on her pink lips. Unable to stop himself, he leaned toward her as one hand slid up her arm.

"You're right." He lowered his head toward hers slowly, giving her plenty of time to pull away. But she didn't move.

Their lips touched and red-hot desire shot through his body. Against his, her lips were soft and initially her kisses remained tentative. Soon she grew bolder and when she opened her mouth Christopher didn't pause before slipping his tongue inside. She tasted like red wine, chocolate and something uniquely Sara. As their tongues met a tiny voice in his head reminded him that he should back away. Jake's sister was off limits. His body didn't care however. It had wanted to kiss Sara like this ever since he saved her from her ex-boyfriend at the fundraiser. No... correction... he wanted to do this ever since they'd awakened in Hawaii together.

Twisting his body he let himself fall back onto the sofa cushions bringing Sara down on top of him. With her entire length stretched out on him, he let his hands travel up her back before sinking into her thick blonde hair. Slowly, he worked her hair free of its ponytail. Her hair felt like strands of silk across the tops of his hands. With his hand he brushed her hair off to one side baring her long slender neck to him. Then he left a trail of kisses from her lips across her jaw and down her neck. She moved against him, causing his already aroused body to harden further, and he groaned before he could stop himself. At the sound, Sara's whole body tensed against his.

"Christopher." Her voice seemed to come from far away. "Christopher, please stop."

A bucket of ice-cold water couldn't have done any better job dousing the flames of desire in his body than the sound of fear in her voice.

While she moved back into an upright position the only other sounds in the room were the television and the ring tone from her phone.

"I don't..." Sara began at the same time Christopher spoke.

"What's the..."

Sara tucked her hair behind her ears and smiled shyly at him. "Go ahead."

The desire that had started to subside a minute before reignited when he saw her state of dishevelment. Her hair hung loose, her lips were red and swollen and her shirt looked as if it hadn't ever seen an iron. *Talk. She wants to talk.* He recited the words over in his mind.

"What's the matter?" He kept his eyes locked on her face so he could catch anything her expression might give away.

She looked everywhere but at him. Then after darting her tongue across her bottom lip she spoke. "I'm not sure this..." Her voice shook. "We got a little carried away once before."

Christopher nodded, unsure of what she wanted to hear from him. Assuming she wanted to hear anything at all.

"Don't get me wrong, I've thought about you a lot since that night in Hawaii, but you're my brother's best friend." She came to her feet. "We're both already avoiding Jake."

How did she know he'd been avoiding Jake? Had he said something to Sara? Christopher raked a hand through his hair. A big part of him told him she was right. They should refrain from getting involved with each other. Yet despite knowing what they should do, he wanted to explore this thing between them. A physical attraction obviously existed. At least on his end and he guessed on her end as well, if her actions were anything to go by. But this was more than just a physical thing for him. The woman he was getting to know intrigued him, and he wanted to discover more.

"I've already messed up my relationship with Callie and Dylan. I don't want to mess things up with Jake for either of us." Her voice caught for a second and he thought she might cry.

Needing to comfort her as well as touch her again, he reached for her hand and pulled her down next to him. "We can end this right now if you want. After we finish the commercial we can go our separate ways. Your brother never needs to know anything happened between us." His mind searched for its own decision. "Or we can see what happens and tell Jake if and when we're ready." Doing so would not be an outright lie but more an omission of all the details.

Sara leaned back against the sofa, her face a mask of worry and uncertainty.

"You don't need to decide now. We're going to be here for a few days. Think about it."

"Thank you." She smiled and laid her hand over his.

The warmth from her hand seeped through his skin and spread up his arm. "For what?" His entire body hummed with excitement.

"Understanding," she said, her gray eyes meeting his, "not pushing."

He held her gaze, unable to look away. In her eyes he could see sadness and insecurity. The night of the wedding he thought he saw it too, but later dismissed it as his imagination. Tonight he couldn't. It was as clear to him as a neon sign. The why and how of it eluded him though.

"It's late and we have an early morning. I'm going to head out." Christopher slipped his hand out from under hers. The constant physical contact, combined with her rumpled state, made it difficult for him to remember why they'd stopped kissing. "Do you want to drive over to the studio together in the morning?" With her hands no longer over his, the warmth he'd felt moments ago disappeared.

The corners of Sara's mouth lifted up to a half smile. "Sure. Meet me here around nine."

"See you then," he said walking to the door.

Christopher stripped off his clothes leaving them where they fell on the floor. He needed an ice-cold shower. Well either that or Sara Sherbrooke in his bed. Since the second wasn't happening tonight, the shower would have to suffice.

Cold streams of water pelted his body from the numerous shower jets. Goosebumps instantly formed on his skin, yet the desire gripping his body refused to disappear. Gritting his teeth he reached for the soap. What had he been thinking? He never should've kissed her again tonight. Not only did he jeopardize his friendship with her brother but he put their working relationship at risk. If they were going to work on this education initiative together they needed an amiable relationship.

As he turned to rinse the soap from his chest, the memory of her face when she put an end to their kissing emblazoned on his mind. She looked just as torn as he felt. And as much as he wanted to continue their make-out session, he knew they would both regret it in the morning. It'd be better for both of them if they didn't get involved. Only one problem with that—his desire to know her better combined with his physical attraction to her was making it almost impossible to make a rational decision. Part of him hoped she'd be the rational one and tell him to back off. Then the whole thing would be out of his hands.

What if she said just the opposite? What if she decided they should see where things go? Most men would say he'd be a fool to say no. Sara Sherbrooke was the total package. If she was any other woman he'd agree. However, they weren't the only two involved.

Christopher let the cold water run over his face before turning it off. Now that his body no longer felt as if it might explode, he wrapped a gray bath towel around his waist and went back to his room. He dressed in a pair of shorts, then grabbed a glass of bourbon from the bar and settled himself in front of the television. With so many things running through his head, he knew sleep wouldn't be coming anytime soon. A movie with a lot of action and some violence would pass the time nicely.

Chapter 6

The reflection that stared back at her told the world exactly what she wanted it to believe. She was a confident woman who had everything she wanted. What would the world think if it knew the truth? Sure, she possessed all the material items a person could want and had a family that loved her even if they didn't always take her ambitions seriously. While her father and brothers supported her political aspirations, her mom believed she should be the wife of a politician not a politician herself. As far as being confident, well that was a relative term. In some areas of her life confidence flowed through her, and in others, insecurities plagued her, especially when it came to relationships. Too many times in the past she'd been burned, the worst being at the hands of

Phillip. Memories of how he'd used her made her cringe. She should have seen through his ruse. Thank goodness she learned the truth before he could damage her father's campaign.

I don't need to worry about that with Christopher, do I? He didn't need money and if he wanted connections he already had them with Jake. If he wanted to see where things went between them, he must be attracted to her. Nothing else made sense.

Regardless, she didn't know if getting involved with him was such a good idea. Before she made any decisions, she needed to consider Jake. How would a relationship with Christopher impact her relationship with him? How about Christopher and Jake's friendship? What kind of effect might it have on that?

Frustrated by her indecision, Sara dabbed more concealer on the dark circles under her eyes. Last night after Christopher left, she went to bed but sleep refused to come until sometime around three that morning. Now she needed to hide the evidence of her sleepless night before Christopher arrived.

Once satisfied with her eyes, she covered her lips with a pale pink lipstick. "Not perfect but it will do," Sara said to her reflection in the bathroom mirror. With nothing else to do but wait, Sara fixed herself some hot tea and reviewed her email.

Just before nine o'clock, a knock on the door pulled her attention from the email on the screen. *Christopher.* They'd agreed to meet at nine, and he wasn't the late type. In one fluid movement she pushed back her chair and closed her laptop, a sense of anticipation surging through her body. When had she last felt that?

Sara pulled open the door without looking through the peephole. "Good morning. I'm all ready to go, just need to grab my things." She turned on her heel before he could answer. Sara wanted to leave as soon as possible. If they stayed in the room they might return to last night's conversation. Something they needed to address at some point, but not now. First, they needed today's business out of the way. Then they could discuss things between them.

"We have time. No need to rush."

Sara looked over her shoulder at him. Today he wore a black Armani suit, the same style Jake favored, with a light blue dress shirt and striped tie, and as he stood there with his legs braced slightly apart and his hands in his pockets, she was once again struck by how much he'd changed since their first meeting years ago. Nothing from his appearance back then even hinted at the gorgeous man he was now.

"I like to be early. It's safer that way." In fact she couldn't recall an instance when she hadn't been early. It was simply the norm for her and everyone knew it.

Christopher opened the door when she approached. "Okay. I don't have a problem with that."

Sara expected him to lead her to a limo outside, but instead he opened the door to a midnight blue Maserati. "Did you buy this for your parents too?" she asked when he slid behind the wheel.

Christopher laughed. "Not exactly. I keep it in LA to use when I'm here. I've only convinced my father to try it once." He shifted the car into first gear. With ease he moved into traffic on the road. "He says it makes him nervous. He'd rather stick with his pickup. I keep telling him he doesn't know what he's missing," he said as he accelerated and switched lanes.

She agreed with Christopher there. At the same time, she admired that his parents hadn't changed as their son's economic status grew. Or at least it sounded as if they hadn't.

"Did you hear back from Senator Healy?"

Sara tapped her fingers against the leather portfolio on her lap. "He liked the changes. Said we should proceed as we see fit." She never doubted that he'd agree. He had never ignored her suggestions since she'd been working for him.

"Excellent. I think we'll get this wrapped up quickly then." Christopher stopped at a red light and looked over at her, his eyes dropping to her fingers.

She followed his gaze and asked, "Are you anxious to get home?" An unexpected stab of pain shot through her chest. Had she read him wrong last night? Was he only looking for another couple nights of sex and used the line about giving her time as a way to soften her up? Maybe he thought she'd be more agreeable if he appeared to be a gentleman?

"It's not that, though LA isn't my favorite place. I thought the sooner we finished this, the sooner people learn about this new education initiative."

His answer washed away her concerns. Los Angles had never been one of her favorite cities either. True it had fabulous shopping but she much preferred New York or Washington overall if talking about US cities, though she couldn't pinpoint exactly why. "What is your favorite place?"

"Depends on the time of year, but overall I'm not a huge fan of cities." Christopher turned his gaze to the road.

Thanks to the image he'd cultivated over the last few years, she'd expected him to say New York or maybe London so his answer surprised her. "I love the city. You can always find something to do," Sara admitted. "But it is nice to get away from it too."

When they entered Bruce Gordon's office forty minutes later his entire team had gathered around the conference table. He was a well-known executive who worked on ad campaigns for several senators and representatives as well as the previous president, she'd expected someone older. She guessed Bruce was only in his mid-to-late forties. Yet, there was no denying the authority he held. There was also no missing the fact that he thought very highly of himself and assumed everyone shared his opinion.

"With some adjustments we can work these ideas in," Bruce said, his arm brushing against hers again.

Sara tried to inch away a little farther without moving onto Christopher's lap. Already she'd moved away from Bruce while she explained the changes they wanted. The first time his arm touched hers, she considered it an accident. But it happened too many times now for it to be accidental, especially considering the space between them. The fabric of Christopher's pants slid against Sara's legs as she angled closer to him. *He must think I'm nuts. I'm practically sitting on his lap?* She'd have to explain later.

"How long will it take?" Christopher asked, his voice all business. The more carefree tone he'd used when he picked her up disappeared the minute they walked into Gordon's office.

"A day. Perhaps two. We should be able to start shooting on Thursday as planned."

Sara liked it when everything ran smoothly. From the sound of it, even with the changes everything was right on track. "I will let Senator Healy know." She scanned the questions she had prepared that morning for the second time. A tiny check mark set beside each one now. "We've covered everything on my agenda." She closed the cover for the portfolio.

"Once the new scripts are ready I can either have them emailed over or I could give them to you over dinner."

It took every ounce of her control but she kept herself from cringing at the suggestion. At least she thought she did. She felt Christopher's hand grip hers.

"We have plans for this evening, Bruce. So email them to Sara when they're done," Christopher said, his voice polite but insistent.

How had he guessed she didn't want dinner with the ad executive? Maybe her expression gave her away after all. Whatever the reason for his interference, she'd have to thank him later. It had gotten her out of what could have been an uncomfortable situation.

By the way she kept moving closer to him during the meeting, he'd known she didn't like Bruce Gordon. Not that he blamed her. In many ways he reminded him of the stereotypical used-car salesman seen in the movies. The man's dinner invitation hadn't come as any surprise to him either. Bruce's eyes hadn't moved off Sara since they walked in. When he'd heard the invitation and Sara's sharp intake of breath, he'd reacted without any hesitation just like the night he'd walked into the ballroom and saw her ex-boyfriend giving her a hard time. That night he'd reacted more out of a need to protect. Today, jealousy fueled his actions. Just the idea of Sara out with Bruce tied his stomach in knots.

Rationally, he knew it shouldn't. She hadn't hinted about her feelings toward him. Still the emotions had him moving in to protect what he perceived as his.

Now with Bruce and his office behind them, he felt more like himself again. "I hope I didn't overstep back there. You didn't look like you wanted to have dinner with Gordon." Before she could open the car door, he pulled it open.

"No, thank you." Sara placed a hand on his upper arm. The heat from her palm seeped through his suit jacket branding his bicep. "And if you don't already have plans why don't we get together."

Her words sent a shot of adrenaline through his system. "You name it."

Sara beamed up at him from the passenger seat, her large gray eyes bright and a full smile on her face. "I hoped you'd say that," Sara answered before closing the car door and preventing him from responding.

A thousand different potential outings went through his head as he walked to the driver's side of the car. None of them had included dinner at the Charter House, an upscale seafood restaurant near the ocean and then listening to a local band play on the beach before a fireworks show. Yet that was exactly what Sara wanted to do that evening. She told him she'd read in the hotel magazine that the band REAL played every Tuesday at Venice. He vaguely recognized the band's name from the popular reality show Do You Have What It Takes. He knew they hadn't won but couldn't remember how they'd done overall.

Since neither had been dressed for that type of outing he dropped her off at her hotel before returning to his apartment where the first thing he did was grab a quick snack. The meeting with Bruce and his associates had included lunch, yet his stomach already wanted more food and dinner was a few hours away. In fact he figured he'd have enough time to eat and get in a quick swim before he went back to the hotel for Sara.

The refrigerator contained a wide variety of items. Before arriving he'd had the kitchen stocked, however nothing appealed to him. He wanted something simple and quick, nothing that required much preparation. As a kid his favorite after school snack had been a marshmallow fluff and banana sandwich. Even to this day he enjoyed the combination. He knew all three items were in the kitchen. Grabbing a bottle of iced coffee from the refrigerator he closed the door and pulled the jar of fluff from the cupboard.

A few minutes later he sat down at the table with two sandwiches, his iced coffee, and his laptop. Email didn't stop just because he wasn't in the office. With the first bite of the sandwich memories of coming home from school and spreading his homework out on the kitchen table flooded his mind. It had been almost a ritual for him every day throughout elementary and middle school. By high school, he'd often go straight to his part-time job or the library after school. With four younger sisters, home wasn't always the quietest place to study.

Halfway through the second sandwich, his phone rang. Christopher's shoulders slumped when he heard the ring tone. Jake. He'd avoided his friend's calls and texts for weeks. He couldn't do it any longer.

"How's it going?" Christopher asked after answering the phone.

"No complaints. You? I heard you're working on an ad campaign with Sara."

He instantly envisioned them kissing in her hotel room after the movie. What his friend didn't know wouldn't hurt him. "We should start shooting later this week."

"Good luck with that. Listen I wanted to thank you for keeping Sara company after the wedding. We all bailed on you two that night, it was poorly done on our part."

Christopher bit back a curse. He didn't need anyone reminding him of that night especially not Jake. "We both understood. No big deal." He leaned back in his chair and raked his fingers through his hair.

"I still wanted to thank you. By the time I rolled out of bed the next morning you were gone."

That morning in Hawaii he had packed his bag and left the hotel less than half an hour after Sara left his room. He hadn't seen anyone except Charlie's mom. Even now he felt a bit like a robber sneaking away while everyone still slept.

"Don't worry, we enjoyed ourselves." *More than you want to know.*

"Good glad to hear it. Make sure she has some fun while she's out there. She doesn't have much time for fun anymore."

Christopher shook his head. If his friend only knew what they'd done that night in Hawaii he'd probably be saying something much different now. "I'll try." And he planned to, despite all the complications.

"I need to go. Next time you're in the area stop by and join Charlie and me for dinner."

After ending the call, Christopher finished the sandwich on his plate. His conversation with Jake only reinforced his guilt over his feelings toward Sara. On the one hand his rational self told him to keep as far away from her as possible. They'd already crossed a line once and managed to avoid any negative consequences. Perhaps they should leave it at that. If they went back to their infrequent run-ins, his friendship with Jake would be safe.

His gut kept telling him something much different. In a way he'd never experienced before, he wanted to learn everything about Sara and be on the receiving end of her real smiles, not just the polite society smile she shared with most people. He wanted to hold her close while they watched movies and make love to her until the early morning hours.

Backing off last night had been torture, but it'd been the right thing to do. Under no circumstance did he want to push her into anything. *Has she thought about it today?* Christopher pushed back from the table. He had more than two hours to kill before he went to pick her up. Would she have an answer for him tonight? Or would she pretend their conversation never happened? Only time would tell.

☙❧

Multicolored lights from the stage flashed over the crowd as the sound of an electric guitar riff filled the night air. Prepared for the show, Christopher turned so his back rested against the stone wall. The popular LA based band played everything from classic Elvis songs to top-forty hits as well as their own songs. People gathered on the park grass and sidewalk to listen and dance as the group moved from one song to the next. Christopher could see why they'd done so well on the reality show. Not only were the members of the band musically talented, but they also had great charisma with the crowd.

Next to him Sara swayed to the music. Every once in a while her arm brushed against his. Since the music began they hadn't spoken, but he never forgot that she was there. And he wasn't the only male present who knew Sara was at the show. So far he'd seen countless men look over in her direction. Some just passed an approving glance over her. Others outright ogled her. Whether they did it because they recognized her or because she was a beautiful woman he didn't know. Their attention accomplished one thing though. It had him looking in her direction repeatedly. From her outward appearance, Sara seemed oblivious to the attention she got from the men in the crowd.

Perhaps she was used to it. It'd probably been happening to her all her life. Maybe she'd learned to ignore it.

On the stage the group launched into what sounded like a remake of a classic rock ballad, the first slow song they played all night.

"I love this song. They performed it on Do You Have What It Takes." Sara turned toward him.

"Interested in a dance then?" He didn't love to dance but he wasn't above using the opportunity as an excuse to get her in his arms again. He still could remember exactly how it felt when they danced in Hawaii.

Sara stepped toward him and took his hand. "Love to."

He led them into the crowd where other couples danced. Wrapping his arms around her waist he pulled her toward him as they began to move to the music. "This sounds a lot like a Foreigner song," he said as they moved to the music.

"Foreigner?"

"You've never heard of them?" He pulled back to look at her.

Sara shook her head and Christopher decided that at some point he needed to instruct her on classic rock bands. But now wasn't the time. As the lead singer's words filled the air, he felt her body come in contact with his. He was uncertain whether she'd moved closer or he had. Honestly he didn't care. He liked the way she felt pressed against him. Having her in his arms felt natural. Gradually, one slow song flowed into another, and neither made any effort to move. Even when the band switched and played their last song, one with a faster beat, neither immediately moved. As the lead singer's vocals blasted over the crowd, Christopher dropped his hands and took a step back.

"Let's move out of the way." The need to fill the silence between them drew out his words.

Sara reached for his hand and moved toward where they'd been standing earlier.

The crowd around them remained even though the band had stopped playing and started to pack up their gear. Christopher didn't blame the people for hanging around. The ocean breezes kept the temperatures hovering around seventy degrees and a large full moon hung over the ocean. With no clouds in the sky it was a perfect night for fireworks.

"Let's go for a walk. I know a great place where we can watch the fireworks."

He reached for her hand again and led her through the crowd toward the beach.

"Almost forgot about them," she said softly, falling into step next to him.

Even though they had broken away from the crowd he continued to hold her hand, not wanting to lose the physical contact with her. He already missed the feel of her body pressed up against his while they danced.

When they reached the spot he wanted, Christopher sank down onto the sand and pulled Sara down next to him. At first he felt her reluctance and guessed she didn't want sand on her outfit, however, she eventually sank down onto the sand next to him.

"What did you think of the show?" Sara tucked her legs under her.

"Not bad. Several of the songs were remakes of classics from bands popular in the seventies and eighties." While they did a good job with the songs, he preferred bands that played their own original songs.

"Really? I didn't recognize any of them."

He couldn't stop himself from leaning closer. "Then you don't listen to the right music. I'll have to introduce you to some good music."

The moon provided just enough light for him to see her eyes searching his face for something. "I might hold you to that," she said teasingly.

His eyes dropped to her lips, and he watched as her tongue darted out to moisten them. Overhead the first volley of fireworks exploded, but the sound barely registered through the haze surrounding him. Christopher leaned toward her as if pulled by an invisible magnet.

"Anytime." He tried to remember all the reasons he shouldn't kiss her again, but his brain refused to concentrate on anything except her lips. Lips he had every intention of tasting again unless she stopped him. It hadn't been his plan for this evening. He wanted her to have time and space to consider things. Yet he knew it was now inevitable. Only two things would prevent it, Sara herself or the end of the world.

Another firework exploded overhead but neither turned to look. Both focused only on each other. Reaching out he placed a hand on her shoulder, her skin warm and smooth like velvet beneath his palm. Slowly he pulled her toward him. "If you want me to stop, tell me now." He managed to get out as he lowered his head toward Sara.

She answered with a simple shake of her head.

"Good," he spoke the single word before settling his lips on hers.

Her mouth tasted like the strawberries she'd had for dessert. Wrapping his arms around her waist he pulled her closer. The scent of her perfume teased his senses as she wrapped her arms around his neck and leaned against him. In the night sky fireworks exploded, bathing the sky in color. Each explosion mimicked the ones going off in his head. Needing to deepen the connection, he teased the seam of her lips with his tongue until she opened them and then plunged in. Slowly, their tongues explored and mated while at the same time he dug his fingers into her thick silky hair.

As the firework display approached its finale, the sounds of the cheering crowd gradually penetrated the desire engulfing his mind. He needed to stop while he still could. One didn't make out with a woman like Sara Sherbrooke in the middle of a very public beach surrounded by onlookers. There was no way to know who was watching. So even though it took almost all his determination, Christopher pulled his mouth away and let his hands drop to her shoulders. For a moment Sara's eyes remained closed and her lips slightly apart. When she did open her eyes, he saw the total confusion and he knew the exact moment she realized where they were and what they'd been doing.

"I've been thinking a lot since yesterday," Sara said, her eyes not meeting his.

"And?" He wanted her to look at him, but still she looked off down the beach. Lifting his hands off her shoulders, he moved so they were face-to-face.

"I'd like to see where things go." She reached out and put her hand on his neck. The slight touch had his body craving more but he held back. "But I don't want to rush out and tell everyone, okay?" she added as her forehead furrowed with concern.

For once having four younger sisters was coming in handy. He'd seen his sisters confused enough about their emotions to know a lot of uncertainty and fear lurked behind Sara's decision.

"No one needs to know." His body hummed with excitement. Before he could stop himself he leaned forward and brushed his mouth against hers again. Nowhere near as intense as the kiss they'd just shared, it still warmed his insides.

The crowd walked around them, exiting the beach when the fireworks ended. He let his lips linger against hers for a few seconds but then pulled away while the kiss still remained light. "Do you have to leave at the end of the week?" He knew theirs would have to be a long distance relationship, but since she was already in California maybe they could extend their time together on this visit.

Sara tilted her head to one side and narrowed her eyes a little. He could almost see her running through her calendar in her mind. "I think David will survive for a little longer without me," she said with a tiny smile lifting the corners of her mouth.

Christopher gripped her free hand in her lap. "Good, then when we're finished with the commercial why don't you stay out here for a few days?" He couldn't think of a better way to further develop their relationship. When she didn't answer right away though, he wondered if he'd spooked her by trying to rush things.

"We can stay here in LA or go up to my place in Alicante or head down to San Diego, whatever you want," he added. In the long run it didn't really matter where they were as long as they had the time together.

Sara's smile grew wider. "I'll let David know I'm staying for a few extra days when we finish and we can play it by ear."

She leaned closer again and kissed him. Although not a high intensity kiss, it managed to call up the hunger he barely had contained. Without a second thought he lifted her up and settled her on his lap. If people saw them and recognized them, they could deal with it tomorrow.

Sara pulled her mouth away from his, but her fingers continued to trace the skin on the back of his neck. "Why don't we go back to your apartment? Maybe you can play those original songs for me."

Did she have more than his music collection in mind or was he misreading her? "Are you sure? It's late."

Sara briefly broke eye contact. "Perhaps I can spend the night. On the way to the studio in the morning we can stop at my hotel so I can change." Pausing she dropped a kiss on his check. "But if you're tired and not up for company tonight, I understand."

Not up for company? Evidently she had no clue as to how a guy's brain worked. "I'm not even close to tired. Do you want to grab anything to eat on the way?"

Chapter 7

By Saturday night the commercial was complete. It had taken several attempts but Sara believed it was exactly what the senator wanted. Thanks to the talented scriptwriters and the minor adjustments she and Christopher made it truly seemed to explain the importance of the new education initiative and at the same time it managed to urge citizens, regardless of their backgrounds or political views, to contact their own senators and tell them how much they wanted it to pass without sounding as if they were begging the American public. Sara felt confident that this new education plan spearheaded by the senator would pass and solidify his run for a second term.

As she packed, Sara thought about her last few days. While this was not the first ad campaign she had recorded, it had been the most enjoyable. Not because of the work itself but because of the company involved. Every morning they had breakfast together before heading to the studio. Once they completed work for the day, they spent the rest of their free time together. Once they took a drive along the coast. Then another day they spent a few hours on the beach. Each evening they either went back to her hotel room or his apartment for the night. While they spent their nights together, Christopher still focused his attention on learning more about her and sharing information about himself. With him it wasn't just about the physical part of their new relationship. While she enjoyed that aspect, she loved that he genuinely wanted to learn more about her.

And she had a few more days of that to look forward to. This afternoon they were flying up to his place in Alicante, a small town located about an hour from Sacramento. The thought of spending more time with Christopher sent nervous excitement through her body. She wanted to see where things went between them, but even her excitement couldn't wipe out the apprehension she felt. Nothing she learned so far told her she couldn't trust him. Still she continued to hold back a part of herself. She never suspected anything with Phillip either, not until the very end. If she missed the deceit of one man before, it stood to reason she might miss it again.

The best solution as she saw it was not to fall in love too quickly. With Phillip it had been the textbook whirlwind romance. If she fell in love again, she planned to take her time and really get to know the man. So far she figured she was accomplishing that goal nicely.

❦

Outside the plane window, the world passed by as the jet taxied down the runway. Sara gripped the armrests and squeezed her eyes shut. In no time they'd be in the air. Planes took off amazingly quickly, though it felt like forever to her. She felt a slight push into the seat as the plane picked up speed.

"I talked to Jake, did I tell you?"

Her eyes flew open at Christopher's question, all thoughts of the takeoff gone. "Um, no." She knew the two would talk eventually, she just hadn't expected it to happen this week.

"He told me you don't have enough fun."

She felt the plane tilt as the wheels left the ground and kept her gaze averted from the window, staring straight at

Christopher. "I'm not sure I like you two talking about me."

He shrugged one shoulder his face expressionless. "Nothing for you to worry about. I told him how we slept together after his wedding and that I'm whisking you away to my private bachelor pad."

Sara's mouth dropped down toward her knees. They agreed not to tell anyone about that night. Her brain searched for the right words to express her outrage. "How could you..." Was he smiling at her? The dimple she noticed before in his cheek now teased her. "You're joking?"

"The takeoff is over."

He remembered how much she hated flying, especially the takeoffs and landings. Her heart swelled. Even her own family forgot how much she hated it. "Thank you." Her face burned with embarrassment. "I think." She didn't like people to see her weakness.

"I did talk to him though. He suggested I make sure you have fun while you're out here."

The way he looked at her when he said fun sent a shiver down her spine and she knew the type of fun Christopher had in mind was not what her brother meant.

"He also apologized for bailing on us after the wedding." Christopher's voice took on a more serious tone. "I don't know about you, but I'm not sorry he did "

They hadn't spoken much about that night since it happened, and Sara rather liked it that way. She didn't think she could put her feelings about that night into a single sentence. "No, of course not." The answer flew from her mouth. "But he doesn't need to know about it." *Or about them now.* It felt wrong to keep it a secret from Jake, but at the same time she didn't want to mess up their relationship for something that may end in a few weeks.

"He thinks you're flying back to Washington after we finish the commercial." Once again he seemed able to read her mind.

"You scared me for a minute. I don't want him to ever know what happened in Hawaii," Sara said. At some point in the future Jake may need to know about their relationship but he would never need to know she'd slept with Christopher after his wedding. That ranked too high on the embarrassment scale for her comfort.

"He won't find out from me." Christopher leaned forward. "I'd rather he not find out about that either."

Relief spread through her. She should have realized that. Her only excuse for getting so upset by his earlier statement was overworked emotions. Flying always took a toll on her emotionally. "Next time you try to distract me during a takeoff can you do it without giving me a heart attack, please?"

Christopher graced her with a grin. "It worked though didn't it?"

She tried not to let her smile show, but it slipped out anyway. "Let's talk about something else. What should we do this weekend?"

For the remainder of the flight they discussed possible options for Sara's time in California, and not once did she think of her brother or how he might react when he learned about her new relationship.

෨෧෨෧

Why had he asked her if she regretted the night together in Hawaii? What difference did it make now anyway? She was staying with him for the next few days.

Each day it seemed like he learned something new about her. And the more he learned, the deeper his feelings for her grew. His feelings for her weren't the only things that were deepening. So was his guilt. Bracing both his arms on the railing, he looked over the elaborate sprawling garden. It was an unusual feature considering how modern the rest of his estate was, yet when his mom toured the Hampton Court Palace gardens, she had photographed a similar one and he had to have something like it.

Where he came from, a guy avoided dating a friend's sister. And if you did you'd better be man enough to tell the other guy. So far he'd managed to break both those rules. His lack of guts disgusted him. He never considered himself a wimp, maybe in high school he been a bit wimpy physically, but he'd never thought himself the type to shy away from difficult things. This current situation proved him wrong, and the longer he waited the worse it would be.

Maybe he should discuss it with Sara. She'd more or less agreed to keep things quiet about them for now, but she might not fully understand the complications their dating caused him. Perhaps if they discussed it, they could decide how to drop the news on Jake. The way he saw it, the sooner they told him the better.

"Wow. The garden is gorgeous," Sara said alerting him to her presence. "My mom would be so envious."

Christopher turned and stared for half a second. The sun bathed her in light, making her loose blonde hair glow as it framed her face. For a moment he wondered if he was dreaming.

"Everything okay back in DC?" he asked, his mind and mouth once again working together.

"I had a few fires to put out. Everything is okay now." She crossed toward the railing. "Can we take a walk down there later?"

Now seemed like as good a time as any. It would give them a chance to talk too. "How about now?" He took her hand and led her toward the stairs to the garden. They passed through the stone archway in silence. He'd watched the landscapers construct every part of the garden and he could navigate it with his eyes closed. He easily led them to the circle of benches nestled among the manicured shrubs.

Sitting on the bench he pulled her down next to him, one arm draped across her shoulders. For several minutes, they sat like that in silence.

"You're quiet this afternoon. Something wrong?" Sara asked, breaking the comfortable atmosphere.

Christopher raked his free hand through his hair. "We need to talk," he began before realizing how she might interpret his words. Beneath his arm he felt her body tense. "I know we said we would keep our relationship secret for now." This time he tried to pick his words more carefully. "We need to tell your brother. Where I come from you shouldn't date your best friend's sister but if you do, he better know it."

Sara's shoulders moved under his arms as she took a deep breath and then exhaled. "You don't think it could wait a little longer?" He heard the uneasiness in her voice.

"No."

Turning her body, she looked at him. "Do you want to tell him or should I?"

No, he didn't *want* to tell him, but he didn't see he had any other options. It was either tell Jake or end things with her before it went any further. "No, it's got to be me, Sara."

Sara didn't argue, not that he expected her to. It was obvious she had no desire to tell Jake herself.

"You stay out here and explore while I call him." Now that he made the decision he wanted to execute it. Once he did maybe he could enjoy his time alone with Sara without feeling guilty.

Sara's mouth turned downward. "Not wasting any time."

"Make yourself at home." After brushing a kiss against her cheek, he came to his feet. "I'll be back soon."

The walk from the garden to his study was about as pleasant as a walk to the gallows. Regardless of how he felt about making the call he knew it was the right thing to do. Walking into his study, he pulled his phone from his pocket and brought up the contact list.

The phone rang several times before Jake finally answered. "What's up?" Jake asked. "How's the filming going?"

"Finished it." Christopher tried to formulate a good opening in his mind.

"That didn't take long. Sara still in LA or is she already back in DC?" Christopher could hear a lot of noise in the background.

Jake gave him the opening he needed. "She's still in California." The words that came out were not the ones he intended.

"Having some fun I hope, but knowing her, she's probably working," Jake said.

Anything work related was not on the agenda for the next few days, at least if he had anything to say about it. "A little of both," Christopher answered. His decision to come clean with his friend faltered the longer they spoke. "She came up here to Alicante to tour Hall headquarters and meet with Caroline to coordinate some speaking engagements." The more he spoke the larger the hole he dug for himself. There was no way he could come clean now about their relationship.

"Good, I'm glad she didn't fly right back to DC. With all the hours she puts in I wonder sometimes who is the senator, Sara or Healy."

Christopher tapped his index finger against his desk. Now that he'd started the lie he had to go along with it. "I noticed that in LA, but it's her life."

The background noise on the other end of the call became louder and Christopher used that to bring their call to an end. "Sounds like you're busy over there, let's talk later."

"Yeah, I'm out in the field today. But listen, next time you're in the area stop by and visit us," Jake said.

"Will do." A strange combination of relief and shame filled Christopher. His conversation accomplished nothing. Damn, how could he have chickened out like that? He came to his feet. Well, if nothing else Sara might be pleased. She'd been unenthusiastic about the idea of telling Jake now anyway.

Men. It never ceased to amaze her how ridiculous they could be. Sara flipped open her laptop. After Christopher left the garden, she went back inside rather than explore alone. The way she saw it she might as well get some work done while Christopher fulfilled his end of what she decided to call the "man code."

The notion that a man couldn't date a friend's sister without some kind of permission was insane. Did all men really think that way? If Jake had dated one of her friends, it wouldn't have fazed her in the least. Evidently men had their own bizarre notions.

Sara opened her email account. She'd checked it only a half hour ago, but already five new messages waited for her. Quickly her eyes ran down the subject lines. Nothing looked urgent thankfully. Her mind wasn't in the right place to answer important emails.

Why did he have to tell him now? She stared out the window. Couldn't it have waited? A month from now they might decide whatever they thought existed between them didn't and her brother never had to know. If dating was as big a deal as Christopher thought, her relationship with Jake may suffer when the romance turned sour. All their lives she and Jake had been close even when they were sent to different boarding schools. The thought of losing her brother sent icy chills through her heart. Her relationship with Dylan still hadn't recovered fully after her treatment of Callie. And her relationship with Callie was far from normal. With all that, she didn't want to add Jake to the list.

There was an easy way to avoid that. Part of her had wanted to follow that path, but another wouldn't let her. Since Phillip she hadn't felt anything toward a man except suspicion. At least not until Christopher danced with her at the wedding. Maybe it was selfish of her but how could she not pursue seeing where things went?

Beethoven's Fur Elise erupted from her phone on the desk. Her mother's ringtone instantly took her away from her thoughts. Thankful for the distraction, she answered.

"Did you know your brother got married?" Elizabeth Sherbrooke asked, her voice still accented even though she'd lived in the United States for almost thirty years, without saying hello first.

Thanks for leaving out some of the details Jake. "Yes. But I only learned about their plan when I arrived in Hawaii."

"Who else knew?"

Sara didn't miss the catch in her mother's voice. "Callie and Dylan. They helped arrange things. Jake's friend Christopher was there too." She decided not to add that Maureen had been there. Knowing that they'd invited Charlie's mom but not her seemed cruel. If Jake hadn't mentioned it, neither would she.

"I can't believe he did this. He should've had a proper wedding like Dylan."

Irritation bubbled up toward her brother when she heard the sadness in her mom's voice. While she understood her brother's desire to have their wedding private and media free, she still thought he should have included their parents. "It's not what they wanted. And if they could have had you there without the media bandwagon they would've." Despite the irritation, she felt the need to defend Jake and Charlie's decision.

"You sound like your father."

Sara didn't see how that was a bad thing, yet she kept that thought to herself. She listened for several more minutes as her mom talked about how wrong it had been of Jake. During the lecture she remained fairly quiet. For the most part her mom only wanted someone to share her displeasure with and apparently she couldn't do that with her husband. Only when she heard a knock on the door did she interrupt her mom.

"Mom, I'll be back in DC next week. I'll call you then and we'll meet for lunch." She opened the door and let Christopher in the room.

As she wrapped up the conversation Christopher remained in the doorway one shoulder leaning against the casing. She couldn't pinpoint exactly how she knew but he wasn't any more relaxed now than before. Did that mean Jake hadn't taken the news well?

"I thought you'd still be outside." He pushed away from the door frame when she put the phone down.

Sara's eyes followed him as he came toward her, his well-muscled body moving with a nonchalant grace, causing her heart rate to accelerate. "I got lonely so I came in to answer a few more emails." The air around them hummed with energy. Did he sense it too?

Christopher wrapped his arms around her and pulled her against his body. "I'm all yours now."

Sara opened her mouth to reply, but Christopher silenced her with a kiss. Whatever questions she had for him died as white-hot heat shot through her body. Gradually, he worked the hem of her shirt out of her waistband and slipped his hands underneath. Caught up in the moment, she wrapped her arms around his neck and let him lead her toward the king-sized bed. With a slight nudge, he pushed her down on the bed. Coming down on top of her, he used his forearms to prop himself up just enough to not crush her or stop his exploration of her mouth.

The need to touch him sent her hand wandering to the hem of his shirt. Slipping her hand underneath, she ran her hand up his back enjoying the feel of his muscles beneath her hand. Lost in the heat of his kiss and touch, her world stopped when he pulled his mouth away from hers.

"Am I a more attentive host now?" he sounded short of breath. In one smooth movement he rolled off her and onto his side, propping his head up with his hand.

"A little, but there's still room for improvement." She enjoyed teasing him.

A sensuous smile with enough heat to melt her favorite pair of Jimmy Choo heels spread across his face. "Really." He leaned toward her, his intentions clearly written on his face.

Sara licked her bottom lip, excitement and apprehension coiling in her stomach. Every time he got close like this she forgot her promise to herself to take things slower this time. Christopher placed the gentlest of kisses on her neck. Inch by inch he moved up her neck leaving a trail of scorched skin behind as he continued his path to her mouth.

"I hope you finished everything because you won't be getting back to it tonight." He looked down at her, his eyes dark with desire. Standing, he grabbed the collar of his shirt and yanked it over his head, tossing it to the floor. His pants quickly followed.

In response Sara sat up and pulled her own shirt off then reached for his hand and pulled him back down next to her on the bed.

꩜

Christopher's heartbeat echoed beneath her head as she trailed her hand over his bare chest, his skin warm to her fingertips. Pure contentment radiated through her body. If she didn't move from this spot today she'd be happy.

"How did your mom take the news?" Christopher asked.

Sara's hand paused. "Um, what?"

"When I first came in you were talking to her, remember? I knew I was good but I didn't realize I was that good," he teased as he trailed his fingertips up her bare arm.

Even though Christopher couldn't see her, she rolled her eyes at his ridiculous comment. "You think pretty highly of yourself don't you?" She leaned up on one elbow so she could see him.

"You weren't complaining a while ago," Christopher smiled knowingly.

Ignoring the comments seemed like the best recourse. "She took it about as well as expected. It's going to be a while before she lets it go." Moving her hand once again it traveled down his chest over his ripped abdomen and circled his navel right above the sheet. "What about you? How did your conversation go?" The hand caressing her arm stopped and for half a heartbeat he didn't respond.

"I didn't tell him." Once again his hand began to move up and down her arm.

"You didn't tell him? What happened?" He'd been so insistent earlier, and she didn't peg him as one to flip-flop on his decisions.

Christopher frowned as he pushed himself up to a sitting position. "I couldn't tell him over the phone. I need to do it face to face. He deserves that."

"Oh." She didn't understand what difference it made in the long run, but by his expression it obviously mattered to him.

"Next time I visit you in DC, I'll drive over and see him."

"Are you sure you don't want me to do it when I get home?"

He wrapped his hand around hers. She'd noticed how no matter where they were or what they were doing, he liked to be in physical contact with her. In the beginning the constant contact felt unnatural, she'd never been with someone like that. Now she felt empty without his touch.

"No, it has to be me," Christopher said with a shake of his head. "Are you hungry?" he asked, intentionally changing the subject. "I'm starving right now."

If he wanted change to conversation she'd let him. "A little."

He didn't wait for her to continue. Instead he rolled off the bed and her eyes followed him. She loved looking at him completely naked, to take him all in. He didn't seem to mind because he made no attempt to dress. The warmth stinging her cheeks almost matched the heat she felt building inside her as she continued staring. How easy would it be to get him back in bed for a little while?

Before she could attempt to get him back beside her, he pulled his discarded pants on. "You in the mood for anything specific?" His shirt followed and Sara almost sighed with disappointment.

Yes, you. "Anything is okay." Sara kept the sheet tucked around her while she collected her own discarded clothing from the floor.

Chapter 8

Sara snuggled closer and automatically the arm around her shoulder pulled her in. They were cuddling on the couch in his home theater, watching a classic Hitchcock film. It seemed the only movies they could readily agree on were the classics. Hanging around watching movies hadn't been their original plan for the day. They had discussed taking his yacht for a trip along the coast but rain and high winds convinced them a day on the water might not be the best idea. Despite the change in plans, she wasn't complaining. In fact she found their current situation more enjoyable than a day on the water. When she returned home in a few days, it would be these moments she'd miss the most. Living and working in DC didn't leave much time for nights like this. Although even if she did have the opportunity, she wouldn't want to spend the time with anyone else.

Christopher was slowly working his way into her heart. Not only did they share many of the same values, but he was also kind and truly seemed to care about her, not just her last name. He asked questions about her likes and desires and he answered any questions she asked. She wouldn't call what she felt love, yet she suspected her feelings could easily turn into that. And while she knew her own feelings well, she couldn't gauge his. Instinct told her he wouldn't risk his friendship with Jake for a short fling. The two had been friends for too long. Still that didn't mean his feelings ran as deep as hers.

Either way when she returned to Washington their relationship would endure its first big test. Many couples, regardless of how long they'd been together, couldn't survive a long-distance relationship. The stress of not seeing each other combined with the already present stresses of life often proved too much even for the most dedicated couples. Not that close proximity guaranteed a successful relationship, but it did help. Right now neither had a choice. Either they try the long-distance thing or call it quits when she boarded the plane in a few days. And although she hadn't been considering a relationship with anyone a few weeks ago, she wasn't ready to give up on this one yet.

"Are you up for another movie?" Christopher's arm left her shoulder as he leaned forward to retrieve the remote control.

Immediately, she missed the physical contact. "Sure how about a Bogart or Sinatra film this time?" She could only handle Hitchcock in small amounts.

Christopher pulled up a list of movies stored in his library on the screen and opened the classics folder. "Tell me when you see something you like."

She read and dismissed half a dozen titles before something caught her eye. "Sabrina," she said, picking the original Bogart version.

Christopher threw her a "you're kidding me expression" but selected the movie. "Is this your way of sneaking in a romance movie?"

Sara clenched her teeth together to keep from smiling. "I don't know what you're talking about. This movie is a classic. They even remade it back in the nineties."

"The classics can be romantic films too. Ever heard of Gone With The Wind?"

Tossing the remote down he settled his arm around her again. "The things I'll do for you," he said with exasperation before lowering his head and kissing her.

The slow leisurely kiss continued through the opening credits and Sara only pulled away when she heard the first lines of the movie. "Maybe we should save this for later. The movie started."

"Or we can save the movie for later," Christopher whispered in her ear, his warm breath a caress against her skin.

Her heart jolted and her pulse pounded at his suggestion. "We could," she answered in a silky voice. Turning toward him she put her arms around his neck. In response his arms encircled her waist, anchoring Sara against his body as his hands slipped under her shirt and caressed her back. The gentle feel of his hands on her skin sent a warm shiver through her. Jerking away suddenly, he reached for the hem of her shirt. With a quick tug he pulled it up and over her head. Placing both hands on her shoulders, his gaze focused on her face before moving downward.

When his hands moved across her skin toward her bra, she almost moaned. Taking his time he traced the outline of her lacy bra before finally unhooking the clasp between her breasts.

"I think you like teasing me," she said, her breathing uneven.

"You have no idea," Christopher said just before his tongue darted out and licked her nipple.

In response Sara jumped as the intimate contact sent her desire into overdrive. Christopher took his time teasing one nipple before changing and lavishing his attention on the other. By the time he finished, Sara's whole body burned and tingled.

"Now might be a good time to go upstairs." Christopher picked up her T-shirt and handed it to her with a wicked smile on his face. "The movie will still be here later."

Sara pulled the shirt over her head. If his sister wasn't currently staying with him, she'd suggest they not waste anytime and stay right where they were. "Let's go."

"During the movie last night I had a thought."

Sara's hand paused with her tea raised almost her mouth. The tone of his voice gave no indication of what kind of thought it had been. "About?"

"The senator's education initiative. I think it could use a few more heavy hitters to endorse it."

Sara sipped her drink, enjoying the taste of the freshly brewed English breakfast tea. "It couldn't hurt. Anyone in mind?"

Christopher reached for a scone and her eyes followed his every movement. "Your sister Callie. She has the credentials as an educator and the public loves her. She's like a modern-day Cinderella in their eyes."

The hunger she'd felt moments ago died. His reasoning held merit. Everything he said was true. How could she possibly ask her though? While their relationship remained cordial they were far from friends. Hadn't she already explained to him about her relationship with Callie?

"I'm not sure, Christopher. She and I don't interact much except when we have to." Sara took another sip of her tea to wash away the bitterness in her mouth. So many times she'd wished to go back and change her initial meeting with Callie.

"Not even for something like this?" he asked, breaking his scone in half. "Think of how many children will benefit if this goes through." The easy-going attitude that she'd come to know disappeared. "It needs as many supporters as possible. If you ask her, I'm confident she'll do it."

If anyone else asked her, Callie would probably do it, Sara had little doubt. But if she asked the outcome didn't seem likely.

"Imagine the publicity it would get if both the president's daughters supported this."

He made a sound argument. Her father's approval rating was at an all-time high for a US president, and he had blown away the competition in the last election and political analysts already predicted he would win hands down in the next one. People liked him. "If you wanted me to ask Jake that would be one thing, but Callie..." Sara's voice trailed off. She considered telling him to ask her himself.

"Sara, you're both adults. I think she'll put aside any personal feelings for something this important. I'm suggesting you ask her to help, not to become best friends."

For a split second she thought she detected annoyance in his voice but then it disappeared, leaving her to wonder if she'd imagined it. Sara focused on her teacup, Christopher's words swirling around in her head. He might be right. The only way to find out was to ask her.

"I'll try, but I can't make any promises, Christopher." Her stomach knotted up at the thought of calling her half-sister. "Maybe I'll talk to Jake too."

Neither spoke much during breakfast. While Christopher polished off a full meal of eggs, fruit, and scones, she merely picked at the fruit—her appetite gone as she envisioned calling Callie. A face-to-face conversation was out. If Callie couldn't see her, she'd never know how uncomfortable Sara was. And she needed to do it soon for two reasons. If she waited too long it only gave her time to reconsider, and if Callie agreed, they could get the word out faster about her support.

For the remainder of the morning, Sara searched for the perfect wording. She knew Callie understood the importance of improving public school education. Callie had been a public school teacher in Massachusetts for several years before moving to New York and the private school where she now taught. But she didn't know if Callie could put aside her personal feelings toward her. During those first few months she treated Callie horribly. She didn't know if she'd be willing to help if the tables were reversed.

She'd like to think so considering what was at stake, but an inkling of doubt remained.

In the end though all the careful consideration proved useless. By the time she came up with a speech and called, that night it wasn't Callie that answered the phone but Dylan.

"Callie's not home. She had to attend an event at school," Dylan said after she asked to speak with Callie.

"Oh, can you can pass along a message for me?" Sara's anxiety level dropped when Dylan told her Callie was gone. "Christopher Hall and I hoped she would contribute her support for the Healy's Education Initiative. It's due up for a vote soon. I could send her all the details."

"Is that the plan Healy worked on with Senator Kenny?" Dylan asked.

Sara didn't recall telling him about it before, but she was glad he already knew of it. "Yes. The senator pulled in Christopher as a supporter earlier this month."

"Email her the specific details. I can't speak for her, but I think she'll do it based on what I already know about it."

The lead weight on her shoulder slid off. She had gotten out of asking Callie directly, and Dylan felt confident she'd do it. Maybe if she was lucky they could communicate about the project through omails, and make things even easier.

Chapter 9

Christopher glanced out the window at the crystal clear blue sky late Thursday afternoon, his lunch untouched on the table beside him. He had to tell Jake this weekend about his relationship with Sara. While he'd flown to DC several times over the past month and a half to see Sara, he'd never once stopped in Virginia to see his friend. But he could no longer procrastinate. This weekend Sara's father had a surprise birthday bash planned for her mom at Cliff House in Newport and he expected the entire family to be there. Sara had told Christopher he could skip the party if he wanted, but going an entire weekend without seeing her wasn't an option for him. Since their time in California they hadn't spent a weekend apart He either flew out to see her, or Sara traveled to his place.

At least Jake already knew his friend was attending the party so when he showed up this afternoon it would be one less surprise for him. He'd told Jake that Sara asked him to be her date for the evening after his most recent meeting with her and the senator in DC. Since Jake assumed his sister was still unattached he hadn't questioned the statement.

While not a complete lie, he'd struggled getting the words out when he'd told Jake the week before. Today his plan was to get Jake alone as soon as they got there and tell him the truth. He'd already figured out what he planned to say. So for now all he could do was wait.

"The plane is making its final approach, Mr. Hall," the flight attendant said.

Christopher looked up from the laptop screen and nodded. The hum of anticipation coursing through his body went into overdrive, canceling out the anxiety in his gut. It had only been a week since they'd been together, but he craved her presence like a man in the desert craved water. How she'd become so important to him in such a short time was beyond him. It felt as if they'd been together for years, not just six weeks. She knew his moods and listened without complaint when he vented. She remembered to have his favorite foods around when he visited her in DC, and she knew how to drive him insane with a simple touch.

Sex with her was incredible. He'd been with women before, but he hadn't known such ecstasy with any of them. Just the thought of what he had to look forward to tonight and his body began to throb. With a groan, he slammed his laptop closed trying to forget how he really wanted to spend the night. Before he could get her alone, he had to get through his conversation with Jake.

Christopher's jaw clenched at the thought of that conversation. Already their conversations lacked usual easy-going banter because of his guilt. What would they be like after today? *I never should have waited this long.*

While he didn't regret his relationship with Sara for a second, he did hate the strain it put on his friendship with Jake who was still unaware. He thought of Jake as the brother he didn't have and the possibility of losing that friendship weighed heavily on him.

On the plus side they would only be in Newport with by her family for two nights. Saturday they'd head to Martha's Vineyard for the rest of the weekend. He smiled at the thought as the jet touched down.

Damn, I'm a lucky SOB. The moment he stepped off the plane and he caught sight of Sara's profile by a black Lincoln Town Car with tinted windows. Still dressed in the business suit she'd most likely worn to work, she talked on the phone glued to her ear oblivious that he was watching her. With her attention focused elsewhere, he took his time giving her the once-over starting at her feet. Slowly his eyes traveled up her bare legs. Legs that he knew for a fact were toned to perfection. His fingers tingled as he imagined running his hands up her calf to her thigh. His eyes continued the trek up to her waist where he knew he'd find a tiny birthmark a few inches from her navel. A tailored blazer covered her breasts but a picture of them was stored in his memory. Today, like most days, she had her blonde hair pulled up in some kind of fancy twist exposing her elegant neck. Later tonight he'd run his fingers through her hair and with any luck he'd find it draped across the pillow next to him in the morning.

He knew hoping for that was a bit of a long shot. She'd already warned him they wouldn't be sharing a room during this visit. Evidently her mother had some old-fashioned ideas about unmarried couples sleeping together in her house. But the way he saw it, what Mrs. Sherbrooke didn't know wouldn't hurt her, so if they remained discreet they might still be able to spend the night together. If not, he suspected he'd be taking a few ice-cold showers during his stay at the mansion.

Christopher got within two feet of her before she tossed her phone into her oversized shoulder bag and turned. He knew the very second she saw him because the lips he dreamed about kissing all week broke into a smile that lit up her entire face. He skipped a verbal greeting and pulled her against him. Hungry to taste her, he captured her mouth with a kiss as she draped her arms over his shoulders. Unable to get enough of her, he used his lips and tongue to coax open her mouth. When she opened for him he thrust his tongue inside, eager to taste her again. At the same time he slid his hands under her blazer. The fine silk of her shirt was soft under his hands, but he knew the skin it covered was even softer. He was about to grab a fistful of fabric and yank it out of her waistband, when he got a brief whiff of airplane fuel. Slowly, their surroundings came to mind.

Kissing at an airport was one thing, ripping off clothes was entirely something else. Releasing the fabric, he dropped his hands from under the blazer and turned down the intensity of their kiss.

After one final pass over her lips, he released her mouth. "I've missed you. It's felt much longer than a week."

"I know." Sara placed a hand on his cheek and smiled. The gentle caress of her hand on his face once again ignited his desire that had been burning all week. If they didn't leave soon, it wasn't going to matter where they were.

"I'm ready to go if you are," Christopher said before pulling her hand off his face to kiss her palm.

Sara readjusted the strap on her shoulder bag and gave him a nod before starting toward the car for the short ride from Newport Regional Airport to Bellevue Avenue.

This was not the first time he'd visited Cliff House, but he was once again awed by the beauty and grandeur of the mansion. While he'd amassed several grand homes around the world, he preferred to keep them sleek and modern. This place epitomized the elegance and formality of a different century. And while his homes may be grand, he could picture raising a family in them. Not so of

Cliff House. He knew Sara and Jake spent a lot of time here as children, but no matter how hard he tried he couldn't picture it. Had she run through the grand foyer and between the marble pillars with mud on her sneakers? Or dribbled a basketball in the ballroom with its gilded ceiling? Neither event seemed likely, so what had she done? He knew she'd left for boarding school rather young, but what about before that?

"I'd say let's sneak upstairs before anyone knows we're here, but I know the Secret Service has already told my father we're here and you need to talk to Jake," Sara said, her voice resigned.

Before Christopher could comment, the mansion's butler approached them. "Your brothers and sister are in the library waiting for you," the butler said in his monotone voice. "I'll have your things brought up to your rooms. Would you like me to show Mr. Hall to his room?"

"No, I'll show him up later. Which room is he in?" Sara asked.

"Your sister put Mr. Hall in the guest room across from yours." The tiniest of frowns appeared and then disappeared from the butler's face, leaving Christopher to wonder if he'd seen it at all.

"My parents aren't here yet?"

"They were delayed. Callie arrived last night to finish up the preparations for the party," the butler answered.

Sara nodded once and then led Christopher toward the library. The closer they got the tighter the knot in his stomach got. How much easier it'd be if Sara could tell Jake herself. Unfortunately, it wouldn't do. Even if she didn't understand why, he knew that Jake had to get the news from him and no one else.

Sara pushed open the door to the library, which he suspected was larger than the one inside his old elementary school. While grand in size like everything else in the mansion, he didn't find it as ornate as the rest of the home. The room's designers used all the right elements to create an atmosphere of restrained elegance and wealth: dark wood paneling, built-in floor-to-ceiling bookcases, and antique leather furniture. A room where you could retire and get lost in a book. Something he'd done on more than one occasion when he'd visited Jake and his family during college. He paused and gently pulled at his collar, suddenly finding it difficult to breath.

A slight nudge in his side told him he'd been still for too long. "Do you want me to come with you when you talk to Jake?"

176 CHRISTINA TETREAULT

Sara asked softly, as they walked toward the other two couples in the room.

"You can't be there."

They both remained silent as they walked and Christopher made sure they never touched. When they reached an empty couch Sara sat but he remained standing.

"Aren't you going to sit?" Jake asked, sitting with his arm around his wife.

"I need to talk to you." Christopher's tongue felt like sandpaper in his mouth. "Alone."

Jake's expression stilled and grew serious. "Let's go across the hall to my father's office." Jake kissed Charlie and stood.

Both men remained silent as they left the room and went across the hall. Although the office was another of his favorite rooms in the mansion, he didn't even glance around as they entered and Jake closed the door behind them.

"What's up?" Jake asked, sitting in one of the two matching leather wing-backed chairs.

Rather than sit, Christopher remained behind the other chair and rested his arms across the back. "Sara didn't ask me to be her date after one of my meetings with the senator," Christopher launched into his prepared lines and watched his friend's face. "We've been seeing each other."

Jake came to his feet and walked toward the huge antique desk in the room. Turning back around he crossed his arms, his gaze focused on Christopher's face. "How did it happen?" he asked, his voice cool and insistent.

Christopher ran a hand through his hair. "We talked a lot at your wedding," he began choosing his words carefully. Jake didn't need to know what else happened at the wedding. "And again at a literacy fundraiser in Providence. Then while we worked on the commercial in California we got close and we've been together since."

Christopher noticed the muscle in Jake's jaw flex.

"So when you said she went to Alicante to tour Hall headquarters and meet with Caroline you lied? She was up there to be with you?" Jake asked, his voice hard.

"Yes." Christopher nodded. "When I called that day I intended to tell you, but decided it needed to be done in person."

"That was almost two months ago." The muscle in Jake's jaw flexed again.

The strike count against him was quickly adding up. "Yeah, I know I should have told you sooner. I'm sorry."

Jake paced a few times in front of the desk then stopped. With his hands on his hips he faced Christopher again. "You're sure about this?"

He knew what Jake was asking. Did he want to risk their friendship? No, but at the same time he couldn't ignore his feelings for Sara either. He'd felt it at the wedding and it'd only been growing stronger and stronger ever since.

"Yeah, I'm sure." The words flew from his mouth. Later he may regret them but for now he had to follow this path.

Jake took a step toward him. "Good luck then. Make sure you treat her right."

Christopher heard Jake's warning loud and clear. "No need to worry."

"Keep it that way and we're good no matter how it turns out between you two." Jake smacked him on the back.

It took some effort but he forced down the sarcastic reply on the tip of his tongue. If the tables were reversed he'd be saying the same things.

"We better join the others," Jake walked over and opened the door.

While he'd rather take Sara aside and spend some time alone with her, he followed Jake back to the library unsure what to expect.

The last time he'd been in a room with Sara and Callie, it'd been a bit like watching two people walk across a floor covered in eggshells. When Sara told him her relationship with Callie was strained he'd thought she was exaggerating, but after the meeting the three of them had with the senator, he'd changed his mind.

"Elizabeth called while you were gone. They won't be here until early tomorrow morning now. She didn't go into details but something came up," Callie said when Jake took his seat next to Charlie.

Christopher felt the corners of his mouth curve upward as he sat down. Would now be too soon to ditch the rest of the family and go where they could be alone? He figured he wouldn't get much objection from Sara. She sat next to him, straight as an arrow with her hands clasped in her lap. She presented a perfect picture of a refined society woman. How long had it taken to drill that society behavior into her? If he were to guess, he'd say years. But she didn't always act that way. During their time together he'd noticed that she reverted to that behavior when she was in a professional or society settings and when she was emotionally uncomfortable. When they were alone she relaxed. She'd slouch on the sofa watching television or rest her head in her hand while she read a book.

He draped an arm across her shoulders for moral support and waited to see where things went.

"What about the party tomorrow? Is it still on?" Jake asked.

A canceled party, he liked the sound of that. Then they could spend all their time alone at his place.

"Warren said to keep everything as planned," Callie answered, confused eyes darting back and forth between Christopher and Sara. "Even if they don't get here until the afternoon, the party isn't until seven."

So much for an easy out. He'd have to settle for sharing Sara for part of the weekend.

"Looks like you're stuck here with the rest of us, Hall," Jake said, one eyebrow cocked knowingly.

Jake sounded like he always did. Christopher couldn't detect any anger or coldness in his friend's voice. "Speak for yourself Sherbrooke. I don't consider myself stuck here." The muscles in his body relaxed and for the first time he noticed how tense he'd been.

"The others might believe that, but I know you too well."

Charlie nudged Jake in the side. "Leave him alone." Leaning toward him she whispered something in his ear.

Christopher didn't hear the question but he was confident he knew it.

"I'll explain later," Jake replied before asking Dylan about the progress on the new home he and Callie were constructing in Connecticut.

An hour easily passed by with the three couples in conversation. Always the business executive, Dylan asked him numerous questions about his company while he and Jake discussed the current basketball stats. He was unaware of the women's conversation but noticed that Sara added little to it. Instead Callie and Charlie seemed to be talking with each other while Sara listened.

He gave Sara credit though. Despite her obvious unease, she didn't flee. She stayed with the group the entire time. When Dylan said he needed to make a few calls before dinner, Sara retreated from the room with him. More comfortable now, Christopher stayed with Jake, Charlie, and Callie for a little longer before his concern sent him looking for Sara. Prior to this afternoon he'd never seen her so tense.

⟋⟋⟋

Now that was fun. Sara removed her silk bathrobe from her suitcase and hung it up in the closet. Her parents acted as a bit of a buffer when they all got together.

Without them, the strained relationship between her and Callie seemed more visible. Even Christopher's presence hadn't helped. He'd been preoccupied talking sports and business with her brothers.

Dinner tonight would be similar. Wonderful. Tomorrow should be a different story though. Her parents and other family members and friends would make it easier to hide the fact that she and Callie rarely spoke. Then on Saturday none of it would matter because they'd be off to Martha's Vineyard. Even though the island was a short boat ride from Newport, she hadn't visited in a long time. Before Christopher suggested the trip, she hadn't thought about the island at all. Now thinking about it lightened her mood.

Dropping her empty suitcase inside her closet, she closed the door and turned her thoughts to a more pleasing topic, Christopher. Although work kept her busy during the week, he was never far from her mind. When something important occurred the first person she thought about calling was him. She looked forward to their daily conversations because he always managed to cheer her up, even when she was having a bad day. No matter what they had scheduled, they talked everyday since that first trip to California. And while she filled up her fair share of the conversation, Christopher talked about his day too. Sara found that a novel experience. Men that she'd dated in the past had either wanted to do nothing but talk about themselves or had shared nothing.

If only they'd tried this sooner. Who knew where they might be now? Maybe they'd be married and living in California.

Sara froze halfway to the bathroom. They'd been a couple less than two months. She shouldn't be thinking about marriage or anything close to it. Their relationship was too new. True she enjoyed his company and they had fun together but that was no reason to rush anything. Besides who knew how deeply his feelings ran? Over the past few years his name had been paired with several women, so she knew he did his fair share of dating. She didn't think he was a confirmed bachelor like Dylan had been before Callie, but that didn't mean he saw marriage in his immediate future either.

Take it slow. Don't lose your head like before. Phillip's image came to mind and a shudder passed through her body. *No,* this time she'd be extra cautious. She didn't need a repeat of her last relationship.

"Okay, if I come in?" Christopher called through the closed door. At the sound of his voice the mental image of Phillip evaporated.

Perfect timing. Sara crossed the room and opened the door for him. "You're done visiting already?"

"You've been gone a while and I got lonely without you," he said, placing a quick kiss on her lips. "You okay?" He studied her face, the concern visible in his eyes.

Sara turned partially away from him before she answered, "I wanted to unpack. I know we're only staying two nights but I don't like having my clothes in a suitcase."

"You didn't seem like yourself downstairs." Grabbing her hand he gently pulled her back toward him so they again faced each other.

Not a conversation she wanted to have, Sara wrapped her arms around his waist and leaned into him. She knew just how to distract him. "Just a little uncomfortable, but I'm fine now." She placed a kiss at the base of his neck then started to make a path upward.

"I could tell. Have you ever..." Christopher stopped and a low groan escaped from his mouth as Sara reached his ear lobe and sucked on it.

Empowerment surged through her when he couldn't finish his sentence. Pulling back, she looked up at him with a coy smile on her face. "Have I ever what?" She reached for the first button on his shirt and undid it.

By the time he answered she had three more buttons undone. "We can talk about it later." Christopher tried to undo the top button on her blouse, but the tiny buttons wouldn't cooperate with his large hands. "I give up. Either you do it, or I'm ripping the damn thing off."

As if she hadn't heard him, she pushed his shirt open and placed a hand on his chest. Through the cotton fabric of his undershirt, she could feel the rapid beat of his heart.

"Sara." His voice came out as a half groan when she kissed his neck.

"You're impatient. Do you know that?" She'd worn the blouse enough times to know exactly how to work the annoying little buttons free. For a second she contemplated doing it slowly to see how he'd react. She dismissed the idea almost right away. Sara wanted to feel his skin against hers probably as much as he did.

In moments their clothes were in a pile at their feet. Inch by inch Christopher's eyes traveled down her body, making it throb. At the same time his hands caressed her breasts then traveled down her stomach to her waist. "Perfection," he said, his voice low and purposefully seductive.

Sara opened her mouth to say the same thing about him, but didn't get the opportunity. Instead Christopher pulled her against him, then set out to turn her brain to mush as he worshiped her mouth, all the while moving them back toward the comfort of her bed.

With one arm lying across his waist and her head resting on his chest, Sara remained perfectly still content to stay in bed while Christopher slept. During their time together she'd learned just how busy his life was. He wasn't a CEO who sat behind his desk all day while others took care of everything. He thought nothing of flying to two or three different states in a day for meetings. If he slept now his body must need it. Dinner wouldn't be served for another hour. As long as they left themselves enough time to dress, there was no need to rush now.

Then again maybe they could skip dinner. The idea held merit. If her parents were around, she wouldn't consider it. While her mother assumed she'd been intimate with men, she didn't like it flaunted in her face. She'd felt the same way with Jake and Dylan.

How much of a hard time would Jake and Dylan give me in the morning if we don't show up for dinner tonight? Jake would be the worst. He'd always been the one to tease her unmercifully. Most of the time she tried to avoid it. This time, however, it might be worth it.

Glancing up, she expected Christopher to still be asleep. Instead she found a pair of eyes staring back at her. "You're awake." Sara pushed herself up on one elbow.

Christopher's finger traced a path along her jaw. "Your powers of observation are outstanding." He tried to keep from smiling, but the corner of his mouth inched upward.

Without a second thought she stuck her tongue out at him.

"I wouldn't do that unless you plan on using it." This time a devilish smile spread across his face.

"We don't have time. Dinner is in an hour, unless you want to skip it," she said hopefully.

His eyes scanned her face and she wondered what he hoped to find. "I'm fine with either, but I'm guessing you'd rather

skip dinner with the family tonight."
Christopher's expression turned serious.

She felt him place a light kiss on the
top of her head and lost another piece of
her heart to him.

"I'd be happy right here all weekend."
He tightened his hold around her. "I don't
think I'm the reason you want to stay up
here though. You looked pretty
uncomfortable in the library."

Damn. She thought she'd done a good
job of not showing how she felt today.
"You know about my relationship with
Callie." The hand gliding down her arm
left a path of heat in its wake, which
started to spread through the rest of her.

"Have you tried apologizing? Maybe if
you sit down with her and explain
everything, you can clear the air between
you." His tone contained a degree of
warmth and concern.

Not him too. Did her brother and
Christopher realize what they were
asking? Sara sat up, the heat she'd felt
moments before gone. Sure she could
apologize, but what if it didn't matter to
Callie? Then not only would she have
made a fool of herself, but one more
person would know how stupid she'd
been. Who would want to open
themselves up like that?

"Now you sound like Jake."

Christopher moved so he sat alongside her, his back leaning against the headboard. "Don't tell him I said this, but sometimes he has a good idea. Not often of course, maybe once a year."

Suddenly the blanket on the bed became the most fascinating thing she'd ever seen. "What if she doesn't forgive me? That would be humiliating."

"It's possible. But what if she does? What do you have to lose by trying? A lifetime of afternoons like today?"

What she wouldn't give for a smart reply. "I'll think about it. I'm not promising anything."

"I won't mention it again unless you bring it up." Christopher covered her hand with his.

Sara breathed a mental sigh of relief, once again appreciative that he never pushed his views or desires on her. While he may voice both so far he always left it at that—a rare quality in successful, powerful men. Or at least the ones she knew.

"So what do you say? Should we skip dinner or not?" he asked, his index finger slowly drawing a line up her arm.

For a moment she paused and again considered the hard time her brothers would likely give her in the morning. In this case anything they dished out would be worth it for more alone time with Christopher. "Let's skip it. Why don't we relax here for a little longer and you can tell me what Jake said. Then later we can head out somewhere for dinner—maybe The Spiced Pear."

"Sounds like a plan," Christopher agreed before recounting his conversation.

Chapter 10

The Sherbrookes sure knew how to throw a party. Over the years he'd attended a few New Year's Eve parties at Cliff House, but it'd been at least three years since the last one. Judging by the scene around him, they put just as much effort into every party they had. The only difference between tonight's party and the ones he'd attended before was the size. Tonight only fifty to sixty people filled the home, while on New Year's Eve the numbers swelled closer to two hundred.

Christopher sipped his champagne and surveyed the guests in the grand ballroom. He recognized several from past parties. The Sherbrookes were a large family that still remained close. In addition to members of their family, Elizabeth's parents and siblings from

England had flown over for the party. Add to that mix some key political figures and powerful CEOs and you had a room full of people worth several billion dollars. If someone had told him twenty years ago he'd be at parties like this he would've thought they were joking.

His eyes settled on Sara across the room. Deep in conversation with her cousin Allison Sherbrooke, she didn't immediately see him watching her. When she finally looked over and saw him, she smiled. Then she said something to her cousin and started toward him, the smile still on her face.

He couldn't tear his eyes away as she walked. Since making his first million, he'd dated several beautiful women including actress Riley Walker, but none could hold a candle to Sara, both on the inside and outside. Right then all he wanted was to take her upstairs, ditch the dress she wore, and show her how much he loved her.

Loved? For a second he stopped breathing. He never doubted loved existed. His parents were an excellent example of two people who loved each other a great deal. And unlike many of his friends, he never went out of his way to avoid it. He just thought it happened gradually over time, not in less than two months. Now that he'd labeled the feelings he had for Sara, he couldn't think of it as anything else. What he felt went beyond a simple physical attraction.

This new revelation put a whole different spin on things and until he grew accustomed to the idea, he planned to keep the information to himself.

"What are you smiling at?" Sara asked when she reached his side.

"You, and how much I am looking forward to spending the rest of the weekend away from here." Christopher leaned closer and whispered in her ear, "How about we go upstairs so I can help you out of that dress."

Standing so close, he couldn't resist kissing her. But, aware of his surroundings, he kept the kiss gentle and hoped it would be enough to tempt her upstairs. "What do you say?" he asked, pulling back.

Sara took a champagne flute from the uniformed waiter that walked by. "My brothers gave me a hard enough time this morning because we skipped dinner last night. I don't want to hear anymore from them."

He watched her raise the glass to her mouth, jealous that she didn't have her lips on his instead. "You need to grow thicker skin."

One bare shoulder rose in a gentle shrug. "You don't have brothers, you have no idea how relentless they are, but we can dance. The band is scheduled to start up again in a few minutes."

While not what he had in mind, it would do for now.

When the band started their next set, he led her onto the dance floor. Other guests cast glances in their direction as Christopher pulled her close and they began to dance but he ignored them. One slow ballad flowed into another, as the band in the musician's balcony played. Not once did they break into anything with a faster tempo. Christopher liked it. The slower music gave him the perfect excuse to keep his arms around Sara without raising any eyebrows. Even if his behavior was acceptable, after tonight there would be no room for speculation about their relationship.

Several times over the past few weeks, their names had been linked together due to their association with Senator Healy and his education initiative, but speculation regarding their relationship never arose. Tonight though reporters from Today Magazine, a national publication, and the Providence Gazette, a local newspaper, had been granted special limited access to the party.

Between the two they'd taken pictures of everyone and everything at the party, which meant tomorrow their relationship would probably be front-page news.

For the most part he didn't mind. In the beginning the paparazzi had bothered him, but now he accepted it as part of his life. Sara was no stranger to the paparazzi either. Still he liked the idea of keeping their relationship under the radar. Who knew what kind of stress the media might cause? He'd seen firsthand how the media could ruin relationships. Jake and Charlie were married now, but they'd almost split for good at one point because of rumors spread by the media. If rumors started flying, how would their relationship hold up? He wanted to believe it could handle anything thrown at it, but he just didn't know.

Warm, supple lips pressed against his, chasing away thoughts of the media and rumors. "I don't think I said it, but thank you." Sara drew her head back.

"For?"

"Coming with me this weekend. I know my family's parties can be a little stuffy sometimes."

"We can discuss how you're going to make it up to me later when we're alone," he answered, his voice taking on a husky tone.

She leaned against him, her body aligning perfectly with him. "Sounds like a plan."

Tightening his hold around her waist, he lost himself in the feel of her body against his. The music in the background gradually became nothing more than some subtle noise as they moved as one to their own beat. Even if the band switched to a fast-paced song, he wouldn't have noticed or cared, the sense of being exactly where he belonged was simply that strong.

Sara wiggled her toes the best she could in her heels. The last time she'd danced this much had been at her father's inaugural ball. Judging by the guests around her, she wasn't the only one who wasn't used to dancing this much. Several other guests, especially the older ones, were seated in chairs around the ballroom perimeter while a few had even left. Even though her feet bothered her, she chose not to say anything. She'd always enjoyed dancing even if she didn't have much opportunity lately. Not to mention she enjoyed the security and acceptance she always experienced in Christopher's embrace.

"The last song tonight is a special request from the President to his wife," the band's lead singer announced before they started a classic hit by the popular seventies group Montana.

Not this song. Sara gritted her teeth to keep from groaning aloud. Can't Live Without You was one of her mom's favorites. At least the band hadn't covered any other songs by the group. If she had a piece of cake, she'd seriously consider stuffing it in the singer's mouth.

Leaning her head against Christopher's shoulder, she tried to block out the music with very little success.

"Mind if I cut in, Hall?"

At the sound of Jake's voice, her head shot up. Other than the brotherly hard time he'd given her that morning after breakfast, they hadn't spoken much since she and Christopher started dating—a fact that was mostly her own fault. Having been afraid of letting something slip before Christopher told him about their relationship, she hadn't made her usual effort to stay in touch. In fact she'd avoided his recent calls and with the exception of this morning when he gave her a hard time after breakfast she'd avoided him here as well.

Christopher's hands left her body and he took a step back. "Sure, I hate this song anyway." He clapped Jake on the shoulder. "I'll see you in a few, Sara." He moved away from her as Jake took his place.

With little other choice, she stepped into Jake's arms as they moved to the music. The reason for her brother's sudden interruption nagged at her, but she kept silent. If he planned to voice displeasure about the current situation, she wasn't in any rush to hear it. So far that weekend he hadn't indicated any displeasure with her decision, yet that didn't mean it wasn't there.

"You two have been inseparable all night. People have noticed."

She shrugged. She, like her brothers learned a long time ago, that you couldn't control what other people thought.

"How's it going?" Jake asked.

She detected nothing but concern in his voice. *How much should I share?* It seemed inappropriate to tell her brother she thought she was falling in love with his best friend since she hadn't yet told Christopher. "Good." Short and to the point.

One blond eyebrow went up as he looked down at her. "Not very talkative tonight," he said moving them across the dance flow.

If she was still ten years old, she would've rolled her eyes at her brother. "It's very good. Is that better?"

The singer on the stage hit a high note as he approached the final segment of the song and she saw Jake grimace. "I'll never understand why Mom loves this song," she said.

"Tell me about it. No man should be asked to hit high notes like that," Jake said in agreement. Not long after the ear-splitting high note, the music ended for the evening, but Jake remained next to her.

"Before you go I need to know one thing. Are you happy with him?" Jake asked, the humor she'd heard a moment earlier replaced with concern.

Sara nodded, a question of her own nagging her. "Do you mind? Christopher made it seem as if there was some kind of law about a guy dating a friend's sister."

A full-blown smile broke out across her brother's face. "Perhaps calling it a law is a bit of a stretch," he teased before his smile disappeared and his face turned serious again. "He's a good guy, Sara. I hope you're happy together."

Good, he hadn't gone into overprotective big-brother mode. "Thanks Jake, that means a lot to me." She walked alongside him as they moved toward the ballroom entrance. "I was afraid that you wouldn't be happy about our relationship."

"Like I said, you won't find a better guy." Jake stopped just outside the ballroom. "What time do you two plan to leave in the morning?"

"I'm not sure, but probably not too early."

Jake dropped a kiss on her cheek. "Then I'll see you tomorrow."

Sara nodded and watched Jake and Charlie walk away. The fear she'd held onto for weeks disappeared. Her relationship with her brother wasn't in jeopardy. Eager to find Christopher now, she searched for him among the guests mingling in the hall. With the music over, guests slowly drifted out of the ballroom toward either the grand foyer or their own rooms upstairs.

A quick scan up and down the hall showed no sign of him. *I bet he's in the library.* He'd mentioned it was his favorite room in the mansion.

Turning right she headed down a hallway toward the room. Along the way several relatives she hadn't seen in months stopped her. With ease though she managed to keep the conversations short and in no time, she stepped into the library where numerous guests remained deep in conversation including the one man she searched for.

He stood on the far side of the room and instantly her stomach clenched tight with raw jealousy when she caught a glimpse of the woman near him. She could only see their profiles, but she recognized the woman as Rebecca Marshall, Senator Marshall's daughter. The younger woman had a tendency to become infatuated with a man and not give up until she got him. The only man Sara knew that hadn't fallen for Rebecca was Jake. He'd actually gone out of his way to avoid her.

The irrational jealousy twisting her insides slowly built the longer she stood in the doorway. Would anyone notice if she dragged Rebecca out by her hair?

Even as she took a step forward, she recognized her feelings as unjustified. He had the right to talk to anyone, same as she did. But knowing this intellectually did nothing to her unexpected emotions. She'd never felt jealousy like this before. It surged through her body. It made her want to grab hold of Christopher and shout *mine* to anyone listening. *Too bad you can't brand a boyfriend the same way a rancher brands cattle.*

A second foot followed the first as Sara marched across the room. Before she reached them, Christopher looked in her direction. Without any hesitation he smiled, his face radiating his genuine pleasure at seeing her. Just like that her jealousy evaporated. While he might be talking to Rebecca, he was pleased to see her. No one could fake the pleasure she saw on his face.

As soon as she joined him, he slipped an arm possessively over her shoulders and she leaned into him comfortable as both friend and lover.

"You look fine, so I guess you survived the dance with your brother. I expected you sooner though," Christopher said after greeting her with a kiss.

"There are a lot of relatives here tonight. I got a little sidetracked on my way." She ignored the whole comment about her brother.

Rebecca Marshall's eyes flicked back and forth between them. Sara felt as if she was being sized up as competition. *Don't even think about it.* Wrapping an arm around Christopher's waist she reached up to kiss him again. Unlike the peck on the cheek he'd given her, she zeroed right in for his mouth and gave him a kiss that told Rebecca and anyone else watching that he belonged to her.

☙❦❧

Floor-to-ceiling windows lined three of the walls in the third floor solarium providing Sara with an unobstructed view of the ocean as she enjoyed her tea. And what a view it was. The sun had started to set coating the sky with various hues of red and pink that stretched out for miles, and there was not a cloud anywhere in sight.

With a lazy stretch, she sank deeper into the sofa while she waited for Christopher. They'd come up from the beach for lunch, but had only made it halfway through when he received an urgent call from work. While she waited for his return, she contemplated their previous conversation about Callie. For some reason she couldn't get it out of her mind. Could a simple apology mend their relationship? Callie never exhibited any signs that she held a grudge toward her. Not to mention she readily provided her support for Senator Healy's education initiative regardless of Sara's involvement. And while she remained reserved in her company, it might have more to do with not knowing how Sara would respond rather than because Callie didn't like her.

If both Jake and Christopher believed an apology would help, could there be something to it? When Christopher talked about his relationship with his sisters and their relationships with each other a mixture of guilt and envy always rolled through her.

She had an abundance of friends and acquaintances but none of them were close confidants—just Jake and now Christopher. Even when she'd attended an all-girl boarding school, she'd always held back a little bit of herself. When Callie entered their family, it'd been the perfect opportunity to add her to the short list of people she trusted. Instead of welcoming her though, she'd done the opposite. Afraid Callie wanted to somehow use the family for her own benefit, she'd tried to push her away. Even though she'd only wanted to protect her family, particularly her father and his campaign following Phillip's betrayal, she'd been in the wrong. Perhaps now was time to fix that mistake.

Such an attempt might fix the minor rift between her and Dylan too. Although very subtle, there had been a change in their relationship once he and Callie became involved. No one else noticed it, but she knew it existed.

Picking up the teacup near her chair, she took a sip expecting a mouthful of hot liquid. Instead lukewarm tea slid down her throat, taking her by surprise. She'd poured it right before Christopher stepped out and it'd been steaming. The tea left in the cup now tasted like tap water. How much time had passed since he left? Normally she didn't lose track of time. Then again most of the time her schedule was so structured she didn't have time to sit around. Before this relationship, she hadn't allowed herself any down time. Before Christopher she'd planned out every day weeks in advance. Since he'd come into her life, she'd modified that. The workweek remained scheduled down to the minute, but she kept weekends free. Now she couldn't imagine going back to her old way of doing things. Before Christopher she hadn't realized how lonely she'd become. Sure she spent time around people, that was part of being in DC, but being around people you worked with couldn't compare to the joy of being with a person you cared about... whose phone calls you looked forward to each day... who held you close at night while you slept.

Her eyes closed and memories of waking up that morning returned, sending warmth through her. As the scene played out in her mind she saw them in her room at Cliff House. He'd already been awake when she'd opened her eyes that morning; her head was on his chest, one of his arms was around her, and his fingers were toying with her hair.

In that moment she'd felt not only cared for but loved. At least she thought it was love. No other boyfriend had made her feel the way Christopher did. Some had come close. And at the time she'd believed she loved them. Yet the emotions she felt with them couldn't compare to the ones she had with Christopher. In fact the intensity of the emotions she felt this time scared her a little. Frequently she reminded herself to let their relationship grow and develop at its own pace. With emotions so intense however, she often forgot her own suggestions.

Several times in the past weeks she'd almost dropped the L-word during a conversation. Each time she'd covered her blunder and Christopher appeared none the wiser. And while she realized the slow course was best, she wondered how slow was too slow? Should she wait until he said he loved her to share her own feelings? Or should she take the plunge first? It could be that he was waiting for her to take the first step. And if she decided to tell him, how would she know when the time was right?

Yawning, Sara covered her mouth. She had a lot to consider.

⌒⌒⌒

"Hey, are you awake over there?" Christopher asked, walking up to Sara's chair. Sara's eyelids flew open, then blinked a few times to focus. Something she could only call giddiness passed through her. "I'm not asleep just relaxing."

"Sorry, I didn't intend to be gone that long."

She'd grown up with meals and birthday parties being interrupted by business emergencies. For her it was normal. "Don't worry about it. It gave me time to think."

Christopher grimaced as he sat down next to her. "About what?"

"My sister."

"Oh." The tone of his voice told her everything. Not only had her answer surprised him, it also made him curious and concerned all at the same time.

"Do not tell Jake I said this but maybe you and he are right, maybe an apology would help things." As she spoke the words her decision solidified in her mind. Perhaps deep down she'd always known she should apologize, but needed the help of someone impartial to make her acknowledge the fact. "I don't know if she'll accept it but..."

Reaching for her hand he raised it to his mouth and brushed a kiss across her knuckles. Warmth shot up her arm then spiraled throughout her body.

"I don't see her as the type to hold a grudge. She'll accept it," Christopher said with confidence.

Perhaps in other areas of her life, Callie might not hold grudges, but she may react much differently to something so personal. "And if she doesn't?" she asked her voice little more than a whisper. She stared straight ahead. If she looked at Christopher he'd see her fear. Admitting you were wrong was never easy, but when another person's reaction could be predicted it became a little easier.

"Then it's her loss, but my computer-simulated eight ball told me that won't happen."

The thought of Christopher staring at an eight ball, even a computer-simulated one, made her laugh. And with that simple reaction, her body relaxed. The fear that overwhelmed her a moment earlier began to drain away. "Is that a program you created at Cal Tech?"

"No, in high school. Four sisters remember? They loved it for their slumber parties and, trust me, there were a lot of slumber parties at my house."

From previous stories he had told her, it sounded as if the Hall house had been a fun place to live. Almost every story he recounted included at least one of his sisters and his friends growing up. Hearing the stories made her a little envious. While she'd had a childhood most could only dream about, it had been lonely. Dylan was ten years older so by the time she could really interact with him, he'd already gone off to boarding school in England. Jake was only two years older but they didn't share many of the same interests, so often he'd go off and do his own thing. When he turned fourteen he left for school in Connecticut. Not long after that she followed in her mother's footsteps and started attending Roedean School, an all girls' boarding school, in England.

Even if they'd gone to schools nearby, Sara knew camping trips in state forests and cross-country road trips wouldn't have happened. Her family vacations included trips to Paris and London where they stayed in hotels with every amenity imaginable. While those trips had been fantastic, she found the stories of Christopher's family trips appealing.

What was it like to sleep inside a tent at night? Could she even fall asleep on the ground? Even with a sleeping bag and some additional padding, how comfortable could it possibly be lying on the ground all night? People did it all the time, so it must be manageable.

"I want to try camping," Sara said without realizing how out-of-the-blue the statement sounded.

Christopher's eyebrows drew together in confusion. "And where did that idea come from?"

"You." In her mind she began a list of items she'd need. She saw a shopping trip in her future.

"Me? You must have me confused with your other boyfriend." Christopher continued to look confused.

Sara slid to the edge of her seat. "The camping trips with your family you told me about got me thinking. I've never been camping. I've never even been inside a tent." She squeezed his hand. "Let's try it."

"You want to sleep in a tent on the ground?" The look of amazement remained on his face.

"Stop looking at me like that. It'll be fun," she answered her excitement building.

"The ground is hard and bugs sometimes get into a tent. And Sara, you don't get your own bathroom when you camp."

Crossing her arms across her chest, she glared at him. Why was he trying to change her mind? Did he think she couldn't handle it? "If you don't want to come, I'll ask someone else.'" She reverted back to her polite professional tone. "Maybe Jake and Charlie will come with me."

The disbelief vanished from his face. "If you really want to camp, we'll camp. I haven't gone in a while but I still remember how." Gently he pulled her arms apart. "How about the end of next month?" He trailed a hand down her arm. When he reached her hand he brought it to his lips. "Deal?" he asked before kissing the back of her hand.

Most of her annoyance washed away but not all. If he'd only agreed because he thought she'd change her mind, he was in for a big surprise. "I'm going to hold you to it, Mr. Hall."

Chapter 11

Sunday afternoon Sara didn't head right back to DC from Martha's Vineyard as planned, but returned to Cliff House instead. Now that she'd made a decision about Callie, she wanted to move forward with it. If she returned to DC first one of two things might happen, either she would change her mind or drive herself insane trying to come up with the right words. If she went back to Cliff House now, she wouldn't have the opportunity to second-guess herself.

As the Secret Service agent turned the car onto Bellevue Avenue, Sara checked her watch. She'd called her mother earlier to make sure Callie and Dylan were still there. Her mother had told her that they planned to stay until late that afternoon. Sara assumed that meant sometime close to three or four. Since it was a few minutes before noon, she figured she had plenty of time.

Pulling into the garage, the agent parked next to Dylan's brand new Aston Martin and turned off the ignition of her car. Although it was one of the car company's newest models, it looked identical to the previous Aston Martin he owned. If Dylan was anything it was predictable and this car, like all his other vehicles, was jet black with a black leather interior.

Jake's Lamborghini and a few other cars in the garage told her several guest remained. Not what she wanted today. If the conversation with Callie snowballed into an argument she didn't want a house full of relatives witnessing it.

Get moving. She'd put on her big girl panties this morning—she could do this. Sara slammed the car door closed. She dealt with the bureaucrats on the Hill all the time. If she could handle them, she could handle a conversation with her half-sister. No problem.

The further away from the garage she got, the slower her feet moved. When she passed the dog kennel her parents built when she'd been showing dogs in competitions, she paused. Today Lucky, Callie's Border terrier, ran around barking excitedly at her. Without a second thought, she stepped inside to pet him. As she ran a hand down the dog's back he licked her free hand, his tongue warm against her skin evoking memories of Sebastian, the last Beagle she'd owned. He'd passed away the previous year at the age of fifteen and she hadn't adopted another yet. Right now her schedule kept her away from home a lot and it seemed unfair to have a dog if she couldn't be at home with it. Dogs needed plenty of attention, something she knew she couldn't give right now.

Sara gave the small dog one last pet, then stood. "No more stalling, Lucky." The dog remained at Sara's feet looking up at her expectantly. "Maybe I'll stop by again before I leave."

Closing the gate behind her, Sara crossed the lawn and entered Cliff House through a back door. When she didn't find Callie after a stroll through all the downstairs rooms, she climbed the central staircase to the second floor. She walked down the hallway to Callie and Dylan's suite, the cement mixer already churning in her stomach kicking up a notch. When she reached the door, she closed her eyes and took a few deep breaths then knocked. Almost right away the door swung open.

"Hi Callie."

"Sara, if you're looking for Dylan, he went golfing with Warren." Callie's expression remained neutral, not giving Sara any hint of her feelings.

A knot the size of a tennis ball formed in her throat threatening to choke her. Yet somehow Sara managed to talk around it. "I... uh... stopped by to talk to you actually."

Callie's eyes grew wide but otherwise her expression remained the same. "Okay," she answered, her voice drawing out each syllable as she pushed the door open further.

Got past the front door, so far so good. Sara followed Callie to the sitting area where a black leather love seat and matching armchair stood in front of a flat screen television. When Callie sat in the armchair, Sara moved toward the love seat and sat down. Dropping her shoulder bag onto the seat beside her, she looked around and wondered if all the furniture in her brother's penthouse was still black as well or had Callie redecorated. She hadn't visited her half-brother in New York since before his and Callie's wedding.

"Did you want to talk about Healy's initiative? I know the vote is coming up soon."

Sara toyed with the bracelet on her arm, but kept her eyes focused on Callie. "No." Sara moistened her bottom lip with her tongue. "I wanted to talk... uh... about..." Sara paused mid-sentence unhappy with her choice of words. "I came here to apologize... and explain." The words came out in a rush, somewhat blending together.

Callie remained silent not even blinking and Sara held her breath waiting for some response.

"Oh... okay." Callie leaned forward placing the palms of her hands on her thighs.

With a whoosh, Sara exhaled. "When we first met, I acted like a bitch." Sugar coating it made no sense. She'd acted like a bitch, plain and simple. "I was in the wrong and I am sorry."

The words hung over them, the tension in the room thick.

"Sara—"

"No, wait—let me finish." She needed to get it all out at once with no interruptions. "A month before Dad received your mom's letter, I had broken up with a man I'd been dating for awhile. We met at a DC fundraiser. Things got serious fast, or at least I thought the relationship was serious." Clenching her jaw, she paused for a moment. "Turned out he worked for Richardson. He'd gotten close to me so he could dig up some dirt to use against Dad during the campaign. When you suddenly appeared, I thought you were someone else hoping to use the family name for your gain. Someone who could not only hurt the ones I care about but also ruin my father's political career. It had happened in the past."

Done. She'd managed to get it all out. Now came the wait. How would Callie respond? Her expression gave nothing away.

The second hand on the mantle clock ticked by, the only sound heard as they sat and stared at each other. A trickle of sweat and apprehension slid down her back. Had she just exposed herself for nothing?

"That's why you acted that way?" Callie's voice held nothing but disbelief. "I thought you hated me because of the relationship Warren had with my mother. I assumed you saw me as some kind of second class citizen because of who she was, or I guess who she wasn't, considering who your mom is."

Sara cringed. Before Callie voiced her assumptions, she hadn't considered how Callie perceived her behavior. "Honestly, Callie none of that bothered me. Yes, I found the idea that Dad had a child with another woman, a little I guess you could say... odd, but it happened before my parents met. If I made you feel that way, I'm sorry about that too."

She hadn't thought much past the apology and explanation. With that out of the way, how should she proceed? "I know this is all kind of sudden, but I hoped we could start over. Forget the past happened and get to know each other." There she'd extended herself, now it was up to Callie to accept or not.

The neutral expression on her half-sister's face finally changed. "I'd like that. I always wanted a sister," she answered with a tentative smile.

Sara released the breath she hadn't realized she'd been holding. "Me too. How about the next time you visit DC we get together?"

Callie nodded. "And if you're in New York, stop by. I don't think you've seen the apartment since we redecorated."

"I'd like that." A small smile formed on Sara's face.

Relief oozed from Sara, when she left Cliff House ten minutes later. She'd accomplished her goal. She'd cleared the air between them and they'd agreed to start over. Who knew what that might lead to in the future? The possibility that they'd never have a close relationship remained, but at least now they could be in the same room together without the tension. If for no other reason, it'd been worth it. Hopefully they'd get to know each other better. They may never be as close as she and Jake, but they'd grown up together. Then again Jake and Callie were close so perhaps you didn't need a shared past in order to have a strong sibling relationship. Either way, only time would tell.

Ten more emails, the damn things never stopped coming. Even though only a select group of individuals had Christopher's direct email address, there still remained a constant stream of messages. Stifling a yawn, he scanned the names listed next to each one. He doubted any were dire emergencies, but he couldn't put the messages off until morning even though at the moment his mind was ready to call it a day. While his watch said seven o'clock, his body kept telling him differently. It seemed to think he was still on the East Coast. Not that he blamed it. Over the past several weeks he'd done a lot of time zone hopping, and it'd finally caught up with him.

The first eight emails required only short replies, nothing he found taxing. The ninth caught his attention. Opening the message from Senator Healy, he smiled after reading the contents. Both the Washington Post tracking Poll and the Gallup Poll showed that support for Healy's education initiative was high and, while it was not a guarantee that the Senate would approve, it made it seem likely. Just what he wanted to hear.

After answering the last email, he logged off his computer and left his office and work behind for the night.

Less than half an hour later Christopher turned on the large flat-screen television in his media room and plopped down with some heated-up leftovers. One benefit of having his sister stay with him while her townhouse was remodeled—she cooked all his favorite meals. His cook came in a few days a week to prepare meals for him also did a fabulous job. His refrigerator was always full of delicious premade meals he could heat up. The only problem with the arrangement, the cook didn't believe in everyday meals. She made a fuss whenever he asked her to make some of his favorites like shepherd's pie or plain old macaroni and cheese, and when she did make them they never tasted quite right. Somehow she always managed to put some strange twist on them in an attempt to make them gourmet. His sister Caroline, didn't share that problem and she cooked almost as well as their mother. When they completed the work on her townhouse, he'd miss her cooking.

Okay, maybe not just her cooking. Having someone else around was nice. Growing up, his house had always been full of activity and noise. Even in college and grad school he had a roommate. Since buying his first home, he'd become accustomed to living alone. That wasn't to say he didn't sometimes miss the craziness of a full house, but rather that he'd learned to deal with the loneliness.

However, as much as he loved his sister, he'd much rather have another woman living with him. Unfortunately, even if she was open to the idea, logistically it wouldn't work. Sara's career required her presence in DC at least as long as David Healy remained in office. He figured there was a better chance of landing on the moon than of her leaving DC to live with him. With his company's HQ here in California, he couldn't make a permanent move to the east coast either.

Christopher twirled a large amount of his sister's homemade spaghetti and sauce around his fork. It tasted as good as their mom's sauce, which she'd learned to make from his grandmother. After marrying Angelina Hall's only son, she taught her daughter-in-law everything she knew about cooking. Although very different from his grandmother, Christopher could see his mom doing the same thing when he married.

As he ate he pictured Sara in a cooking lesson with his mom. What a sight that would be. So far the only culinary skills he'd seen Sara exhibit involved boiling water and pressing the button on the microwave. Not that he was much better, although he could at least add grilling to his list.

How would Sara react to his parents? One of these days they'd have to meet. So far she had only met Caroline.

His mind wandered back to the imaginary cooking lesson between Sara and his mom. A smile spread across his face at the mental image of Sara standing in his family kitchen making baklava, something his mom made every year for the holidays. She'd tried to teach him once and had given up halfway through the lesson.

Quickly the image shifted. Instead of Sara in his mom's kitchen, he envisioned him and her cooking together in his kitchen. Now that was a picture he liked.

His ringing cell caused the picture to evaporate.

Pulling the phone from his pocket, Christopher glanced at the screen. "I was just thinking about you," he said, answering the phone. "I thought you'd call last night." He'd picked up his phone three different times the night before prepared to call her. She'd never said she would call, but he'd expected to hear from her after her meeting with Callie. And he honestly wanted to know how it went.

"I intended too, but I got home later than expected." She sounded as tired as he felt. She'd been hopping back and forth between time zones almost as much as him.

Christopher leaned back, prepared for a long conversation. Before Sara entered his life, he never did long phone calls. Short and to the point worked fine for him. Long in-depth talks were better conducted face to face. Unfortunately, that wasn't an option tonight.

"How did it go?"

"Okay, I think." Sara's positive reply didn't match her hesitant tone.

"But?"

"Nothing. I explained everything and we agreed to put the past behind us. We'll see what happens."

Sara tried to dismiss the importance of the situation, but he knew the truth. She'd taken a big emotional risk approaching Callie. A risk he hoped would pay off. "That means you have nothing else to say on the matter, right?"

Her sweet laugh carried over the phone and he smiled himself.

"You're so smart. Let's talk about next weekend instead. I think it's my turn to come out there."

With the week stretched out before him, the weekend seemed like a lifetime away. He had so many obligations already scheduled for the week, half of them in Texas. "I'll come there again. I'll be in Texas until Thursday afternoon anyway."

Chapter 12

"You're sure about this?" Christopher asked.

Sara ground her teeth together. He'd asked her the exact same question more times than she cared to count in the past few weeks, and already twice since he picked her up in DC earlier that day. "Positive. I want to try it, but if you want we can get a hotel room for the weekend. I'll try camping some other time. I think Jake and Charlie will come with me."

Christopher reached across the SUV and gave her hand a quick squeeze. "I never said I didn't want to do this with you. But I'm not sure you'll enjoy yourself."

In the end she might hate camping, but doing it was the only way to find out. No matter what Christopher said, she planned to go through with her plans for the weekend. If Christopher wanted to stay in a hotel along the beach, he could. Who knew? After one night of sleeping on the ground in a tent she might be booking a hotel room with a king-sized bed and room service.

"Why did you pick here?" she asked, changing the topic of the conversation. If he kept questioning her decision, her annoyance would only increase.

Christopher shook his head, resigned to the fact she wouldn't budge. "My grandparents lived here. We used to come every other year to visit in the summer. Sometimes we'd stay with them and sometimes we camped. I loved it, and when you said you wanted to try camping it was the first place that came to mind."

"If your grandparents lived in Virginia Beach how did your family end up in Wisconsin?" She'd heard of people moving from colder areas of the country to warmer ones, but it didn't usually happen the other way.

Christopher turned the Range Rover onto Atlantic Avenue. "They moved here after they retired. My grandfather was in the Navy and was stationed down here for a few years. After he left the Navy they moved back to his hometown in Wisconsin to be closer to family."

"Do they still live here?"

"They live in Florida now. They've been down there for three years. They sold their house here to my aunt and uncle."

Sara studied the busy street out the window. Window signs and billboards welcomed visitors from all over. She'd never visited the area but a few of her college friends had. From what they had told her the area had gorgeous beaches and, while not as warm as areas farther south, it remained warmer than Wisconsin.

"Are you up for an excursion or two while we're here?" Sara asked. Across the street a large billboard stood advertising various area attractions including dolphin-watching trips and naval base cruises.

"I thought we could just relax this weekend, but if you have something in mind just name it." Christopher pulled the Range Rover into a parking garage. "Before we do any planning though, let's eat and then head to the campground to set up before it gets dark. We can always come back here later tonight if we want." Before Sara could respond, he got out of the SUV and came around to open her door.

"Sounds good. Lead the way." Sara accepted his outstretched hand and they walked out into the bright warm sunshine.

Buildings of various sizes and shapes lined both sides of Atlantic Avenue. As they walked, along Sara took it all in. People from all corners of life strolled up and down the street. Some were dressed in bathing suits with bodyboards over their shoulders, while others grasped the hands of young children as they made their way to and from the beach with sand buckets and shovels. Mixed in among the city sounds, were crashing ocean waves and the frequent roar from military jets as they flew overhead. The entire scene was as opposite from her last vacation in Paris as it could get. Oddly, she found herself instantly attracted to the area. While it may not have famous art museums or world-class fashion houses, there was something she liked about the area. Something that told her this wouldn't be her last trip here. She understood why Christopher's grandparents moved here after retiring.

"So what are you in the mood for? Seafood, pasta, steak?" Christopher held her hand as they crossed the street toward the boardwalk. "Make sure it's something you'll love. This will be your last civilized meal before we start roughing it."

His expression remained serious, but she thought she caught a gleam of mischief in his eye. He was kidding around again, wasn't he? She hoped so. "We're at the ocean. I want seafood tonight." Farther down the way Sara caught a glimpse of several statues clustered together. "What's that down there?" Sara asked, pointing toward the area.

Christopher released her hand and placed his arm around her shoulders. "A memorial to the military. We can take a walk through tomorrow. We really don't have time now."

They walked a little more before Christopher stopped outside a hotel. "The restaurant inside has the best seafood around, at least it used too. I haven't been here in two or three years."

Sara moved forward and the automatic glass doors into the lobby opened. "It'll be fine."

Two hours later Sara took in their surroundings as Christopher stopped at the campsite inside North Bayshore Campground. Whether he'd requested a secluded spot or all the sites were like this one, there wasn't another tent or camper in sight. The only thing Sara saw were trees, trees, and more trees. Wouldn't it be safer around more people?

If an emergency arose they were all alone except for the Secret Service agents that were with them. She had considered asking them not to come, now she was glad they were there.

"Are all the sites like this one?" Sara struggled to keep her voice even. If he picked up on her uneasiness, he'd start talking about getting a hotel room. No matter what, she wasn't going to give up without trying this first.

Christopher opened his door but remained seated inside the SUV. "Some are but not all. I asked for a more private one. I figured you wouldn't want to draw a lot of attention." Climbing out of the SUV, he closed the door and walked around to open her side. "You can explore if you want or give me a hand unloading. Up to you."

Sara planned on doing this right and experiencing every aspect of camping, which included setting up. "Just tell me what you need me to do."

"Let's get unloaded first. For now put everything on the picnic table." Christopher moved closer and dropped a quick kiss on her lips then opened the trunk.

Without complaint Sara accepted the dark purple sleeping bag he handed her. In the end she allowed him to do most of the shopping for their trip. One afternoon the week before she stopped in an outdoor recreation store, but gave up after an hour in the tent section. There were simply too many options. Tents seemed to come every size and shape imaginable depending on needs and environment. As much as she loved shopping, she asked Christopher to pick up everything they would need for their weekend trip. The only items she purchased were a new bikini and sandals.

"After we set up I need to put more ice in this," Christopher said as he pulled a large cooler from the trunk.

Sara reached for the second sleeping bag in the trunk. "What's that for?" she asked pointing to the cooler.

Christopher stopped and threw her a look that said exactly what he thought. "Umm... food."

Okay, she set herself up for that one. She knew what a cooler was for. "I meant why do we need one. Can't we go out to eat?"

"We can, but that's not camping. A true camping trip involves cooking hot dogs over an open fire. I brought some other food too like peanut butter for sandwiches, oatmeal, plus some marshmallows."

Okay, she could handle a hot dog or two as long as he didn't expect her to eat them at every meal and she did like peanut butter.

"There is also bottled water in here," he explained placing the cooler near the picnic table.

Once they emptied all the gear from the back of the Range Rover, Christopher worked on setting up the tent. With no knowledge of how to start, Sara sat on the picnic table content to watch him work. Christopher breezed through the process and before long he began pounding the stakes into the ground anchoring the tent down.

"Grab your sleeping bag and come on in." Christopher tossed the mallet down on the table. "Just make sure you take your shoes off before you go inside." He grabbed his own bag and a rolled-up foam pad.

Sara reached for the sleeping bag behind her but didn't get any further; her butt remained glued to the bench. Thinking about this trip and seeing the tent set up in the store had been one thing, but now it dawned on her how little protection there would be between her and the wild creatures. She bit down on her lip. After all the fuss she'd made, she had to at least try this for one night.

Besides the Secret Service agents with their guns weren't that far away.

Christopher poked his head out of the tent. "We can still pack everything up and get a room somewhere."

Get up. Sara forced herself into an upright position. "We're staying here tonight." Moving lead weights was probably easier than getting her feet to move toward the tent, but she managed. "Let's see how it goes. We can always move in the morning." Sara stopped just outside the tent and kicked off her sneakers. Then before she rethought her decision she ducked inside clutching her sleeping bag tightly.

Inside Christopher had opened his sleeping bag and spread it out making a makeshift bed. "I'm no expert but don't you usually sleep inside a sleeping bag?"

Christopher dropped onto the ground and reached up to pull her next to him. "There's no way I'm sleeping this close to you and not being able to touch you. We'll open your bag and cover up with it if we need it." While he spoke he leaned toward her. "But I can think of more enjoyable ways to stay warm if we get cold."

The seductive tone in his voice warmed her entire body and her surroundings disappeared. She no longer felt the hard ground underneath her or heard the chirping birds outside the tent. "I think I'm going to enjoy camping," she managed to say just before his lips came down on hers.

Beneath her cheek Christopher's chest rose and fell as he slept. Carefully, so she didn't wake him, Sara rolled onto her back. The tent was so dark Sara could barely make out Christopher next to her. Outside the night air was filled with unfamiliar sounds that other people may be able to tune out, but Sara seemed to notice each and every one. The sounds outside the tent weren't the only things keeping her awake. Even with the thin foam mattress and a sleeping bag beneath them, she found it impossible to get comfortable. No matter what position she tried, it didn't help. Next to her, Christopher was dead to the world. Evidently he didn't share her problems.

Perhaps she should wake him up and together they could find an enjoyable way to pass the time. After their last round of lovemaking, she'd managed to fall asleep for a little while anyway. Maybe it would happen again. In her mind she ran through pleasurable ways of waking him. Sitting up she leaned toward him and began a trail of kisses at his neck. Slowly she made her way down toward his chest.

She got just above his left nipple when an owl hooted and Sara almost jumped through the tent.

Jolted fully awake by her sudden movement, Christopher bolted upright. "What's the matter? Are you okay?"

Sara nodded before she remembered Christopher couldn't see her. "An owl or at least I think it was an owl scared me. I'm not used to all these nature sounds."

"After a while you get used to it." Christopher lay back down and pulled her next to him. "Tomorrow night you might not even notice."

She doubted that. Every few seconds a different sound filtered in from outside, but she kept her thoughts to herself. If she complained now he'd only insist they get a hotel room for the weekend. Even if she went all weekend with no sleep, she wanted to see this camping trip through. Giving up wasn't in her nature and she didn't plan on starting now.

☙❧

He gave her a lot of credit. So far this weekend she hadn't complained once. Not even after last night and judging by the dark circles under her eyes and the fact that she yawned, every other minute she hadn't slept much. Despite her lack of rest when he asked her that morning about changing their accommodations, she'd adamantly refused.

"What are your thoughts for today?" Christopher asked as they strolled along the boardwalk past the enormous statue of Neptune, god of the ocean. "We could look into one of those excursions you mentioned yesterday."

Sara shook her head as she stifled another yawn. "I'm thinking a day relaxing on the beach sounds perfect. Maybe tonight we can come back for the live concert in Neptune Park."

"A day lying on the beach works for me." Crossing to the stairs he led her down to the beach toward an area with rented recliners. Around them children worked on building sand fortresses while their parents sat and watched. Another group played a game of volleyball and others simply sat and enjoyed the warm sunshine. No one paid any attention to them as they walked by, everyone assumed they were just another couple intent on spending time in the sun.

After selecting two recliners far from a group of teens playing Frisbee, Christopher dropped the backpack slung over his shoulder. Unsure of their exact plans for the afternoon, he'd packed sunscreen and bottled water for both of them. "Plan on doing any swimming?" he asked pulling his T-shirt over his head.

Sara's head disappeared inside her T-shirt. Pulling it off, she revealed the top of her emerald green bikini. "The only swimming I do is in a pool. I like to know what's around me." Sara pulled off her shorts and folded them neatly before placing them on the end of her chair. "But go ahead if you want."

Christopher's eyes took in the sight of her lying there in her bikini; once again he was struck speechless by her beauty. By now he should be used to it, but somehow she still managed to leave him breathless.

"Can I borrow the sunscreen?" she asked, adjusting her sunglasses.

Without tearing his eyes from her, he dug into the bag and pulled out the bottle he had packed. "Here you go."

He watched every movement she made as she rubbed the white lotion across her body. With each pass the fire simmering inside him increased as memories of loving her that morning teased him. If he had any hope of surviving the afternoon he needed to look elsewhere. Lifting his eyes he watched two military jets screeching across the sky. When they disappeared into the clouds he lowered his gaze and caught sight of several men watching Sara as she applied a layer of sunscreen to her legs. *Watch all you want, but she's with me.*

"When you're done can I get some help?" he asked, sitting down on the edge of her chair and kissing her cheek. "I'll return the favor."

Sara paused with one hand on her calf and shot him a smile. "I was hoping you'd ask." Moving closer to the edge of her chair she squeezed sunscreen on her hand. "Turn around and I'll get your back."

The nerve endings in his back jumped the second Sara's hand made contact. Her touch felt like a caress as she spread the sunscreen across his upper back and shoulders. Gradually she worked her way down his spine. Instinctively he leaned back into her caress, content to sit there all day.

"Anywhere else you need help?" Sara asked as her hands skimmed across his lower back and above his waistband.

He could think of several other places where he'd like her hands, but none were appropriate for their current location. "Good for now. What about you?"

Her hands left his back and for a moment he tossed around ideas how he might get them back.

"Just my back. I covered everywhere else."

Christopher took his time covering every inch of her shoulders and back. When he could no longer use the ruse of applying sunscreen as his reason for touching her, he let his hand rest on her shoulders and dropped a kiss on the back of her neck. "All set."

In the center of the stones a fire blazed, the smoke keeping any mosquitoes at bay. Sara watched mesmerized as the flames danced wildly near the marshmallow on her stick. "I've never tasted a roasted marshmallow before," she said just before yawning for about the millionth time that night.

Christopher's hand wrapped around hers and adjusted the stick. "Most people like them light brown, but I like them best when they get charred on the outside."

"Maybe I'll try them both ways and with the chocolate and graham crackers you brought."

"S'mores are a must on a camping trip," he said with the utmost authority in his voice. Pulling his own marshmallow out of the fire, he pulled the sticky concoction off the stick and popped it into his mouth.

She watched for some sign that it had been too hot, but none ever came. Cautiously she followed his lead and did the same thing. Despite being so close to the flames, the outside of the marshmallow was warm, but it didn't burn her fingertips. Popping the roasted pillow of sugar into her mouth she bit down. It melted in her mouth and she closed her eyes in delight. "Mmm... that's good." She licked the remaining sticky goo from her fingers. "People must go camping just for this."

Christopher stuck another marshmallow on the end of each stick. "I take it you're not having fun."

Was that disappointment she heard in his voice? "I didn't say that. But next time we need an air mattress and some ear plugs." Perhaps she could learn to tune out the sounds of nature, but the hard ground... well that was something else entirely.

"We can still get a room for the night." He rotated the stick holding his marshmallow.

"Will you stop saying that?" Sara snapped. "I'm fine where we are. I'm just saying for next time." More than anything she wanted to hit him over the head with her stick.

He reached for her free hand. "Okay, okay. I just want you to have a good weekend."

Sara leaned against him. "I am. This trip has been great. We have time alone with no one bothering us. That's all I want." Her friends may find it odd, but she didn't care where they spent their time. All that mattered to her was they were together having fun. So far their weekend camping trip fit the bill to a T.

"Me too." He reached for the bag of marshmallows on the picnic table. "Ready for another?" he asked.

"Definitely. This time I want the chocolate and graham crackers too."

Together they sat roasting marshmallows and constructing s'mores, for another thirty minutes or so then doused the fire and climbed into their tent.

"I need to figure out a way to make those at home." Sara snuggled next to Christopher, the steady sound of his heartbeat under her ear.

Christopher played with her loose strands of hair lying across his chest. "Use the microwave. They taste almost the same."

No longer able to keep them open, she let her eyelids close. "Even I can handle that," she whispered before falling asleep.

Chapter 13

Sara's ringing cell phone pulled her attention away from the opened email on her computer screen. A number with a California area code showed up on the screen, with no name attached. Assuming it was another reporter, Sara ignored the call and let it go to voicemail. It looked like she needed to change her number again.

Prior to her mom's birthday party the month before, she'd remained under the media's radar and they'd left her alone. Since the party, though, every media outlet latched onto her and Christopher's relationship. Pictures of them together appeared on more than half the magazines published that week alone. Reporters tried to get statements from her. They called her office repeatedly and a few had even gone so far as showing up at Senator Healy's office at the Capitol. Thankfully security intercepted and turned them all away before they could get close. Now it looked like they managed to get their hands on her personal number.

Though not the first time the media zoomed in on one of her relationships, they hadn't been this zealous since her short fling with actor Anderson Brady years earlier. In hindsight she should have expected it. Her past two relationships had been with men not known outside of politics. Thanks to his success, everyone knew the name Christopher Hall.

With a half-hearted sigh, Sara went back to reading the email from Senator Healy. The man's messages tended to be long winded. She found that humorous because in person he always cut right to the point. Scanning down the screen, she dismissed the first two paragraphs, which contained a basic itinerary for his current trip. An itinerary she'd established for him.

"You've got to see this," Hannah, one of the senator's interns, said as she came into Sara's office. "Turn to channel 55."

Sara's heart stopped. Hannah never entered without knocking first. For her to have done so meant a lot. "What happened?" Visions of terrible events went through her head.

"Carl Knight and Miriam Walker are on the Brown Report talking about the senator's education initiative." Hannah grabbed the remote from Sara's desk and turned on the television. Immediately Vincent Brown, the host of the popular news talk show on CZN, came on the screen.

While perhaps interesting, Sara didn't see the announcement as earth-shattering. Both political analysts regularly appeared on CZN and even without hearing their latest conversation Sara could picture how the discussion would go. Carl Knight was a well-respected political analyst who normally maintained a bipartisan view. Miriam Walker was more an extremist who found fault with everything Senator David Healy and his party did.

"According to polls most of the country is behind this initiative approved by both the House and the Senate. I've heard it said that it will turn US public schools around. Make them competitive again with the rest of the world," Vincent Brown's voice came through the television.

"I don't know where you're getting your information, but most people in

Washington do not have confidence in this plan. The only reason it passed was because President Sherbrooke's daughter attached her name to it. Without that name, the plan never would've made it out of the Senate regardless of what other names Senator Healy tied to it. And he knew that. Why do you think he pulled in Sara Sherbrooke?"

"Miriam, I have to—" Carl began to say but didn't get the opportunity to finish.

"Now that it has passed who is the real beneficiary? Hall Technology. It was announced this morning that Christopher Hall's company was awarded a very lucrative government contract, which is directly tied to the bill. As you know Christopher Hall was one of Healy's biggest campaign donors, and he is romantically involved with Sara Sherbrooke. There's no way all that is a coincidence, Vincent." Miriam Walker said smugly.

The voices from the television became nothing more than a hum in the background as Sara stopped breathing. Had the plan only passed because of her support? Had Christopher and David used her for their own gains? From the start David had wanted her to publicly support the plan. When she'd refused the first time, he'd let it go. The topic hadn't come up again until Christopher suggested it. Had it been staged? Her mind went back to her original conversation with Christopher. Looking back, their whole conversation took on a different tone.

"I'm glad Hall Technology got the contract. From what I've read, it seems like a great company and is considered one of the top companies in the US." Hannah's voice drifted through the haze in Sara's head.

Sara closed her eyes she fought to control the emotions bombarding her. "I need to go, Hannah. If anyone comes looking for me tell them I left." She stood and grabbed her bag and purse.

"Hey, are you okay?" Hannah asked. "You look pale." Hannah asked.

No, she wasn't okay. "Just do what I said, please Hannah." Sara walked past Hannah without waiting to hear her reply.

༄༅༄

Later that evening an untouched cup of tea sat on the end table. A knot the size of a boulder sat in her stomach and only continued to grow as little details from the past couple of months came to mind.

At the time she hadn't thought anything of it when Christopher said he played golf with the senator just before

Jake's wedding but now she couldn't stop thinking about it. What if, during that game, David told Christopher how she refused to publicly endorse the plan? What if Christopher had agreed to get Sara on board in exchange for the government contract? A contract she hadn't even known he had bid on. True she'd received a list of all the companies who submitted bids, but she hadn't read it and he'd never once mentioned it.

If Christopher had made such an agreement with David perhaps the whole night in Hawaii hadn't been unplanned on his part. Maybe he'd set out to seduce her that night and she'd blindly fallen for it. And what about his sudden appearance at the fundraiser in Providence? Maybe that too had been part of his plan to get close to her so he could convince her to link her name to the education initiative.

Sara pinched the bridge of her nose as memories of their first meeting in DC came to the forefront. He'd suggested and eventually convinced her to do the ad campaign with him. The only reason her name became associated with the initiative was because of him. Worse yet the only reason Callie's name was attached to it was because of him. If not for his encouragement Sara never would have reached out to her.

Sara wiped the single tear that slipped down her cheek and reached for her tea. Miriam Walker was right. Prior to her support many hadn't expected the initiative to even squeak though the Senate. Yet in the end it passed by a landslide in both the House and Senate. That was no coincidence and now Hall Technology was reaping the benefits.

As she sipped her tea, Sara leaned her head back against the sofa cushion. She wished she could turn her brain off for the night. It literally hurt to think. Ideas and assumptions kept going through her mind. Every conversation she'd had with Christopher since that night in Hawaii replayed in her head. Had he used her to get what he wanted? Had his true reason for supporting the education initiative been more about getting the lucrative government contract rather than wanting improvements in schools?

Christopher ran a billion dollar company, which meant he was a businessman first and foremost, but she'd believed he was more than that. At least he acted like more than that. Had she been taken in by another man who wanted to use her for his own gain? She didn't want to believe it, but she couldn't stop reaching that conclusion. All the evidence pointed in that direction. How could she have been so stupid again? Squeezing her eyes tighter, she bit down on her lip. Another teardrop slipped down her cheek and soon she stopped wiping them away.

The doorbell rang a second time, but Sara remained on the sofa. She'd sat in the same spot for over an hour preparing what she wanted to say when Christopher arrived.

When the doorbell echoed through the room a third time she took in a deep breath. *Get up and answer it.* Avoiding him wouldn't change anything. It would only put off the inevitable. With a heavy heart she stood and, with her back straight and head held high, moved toward the door.

"Did your other boyfriend need time to sneak out the window?" Christopher asked when she opened the door. "I hope he knows you're busy all weekend." Without waiting for an answer, he moved toward her removing his jacket.

Sara took a single step toward him before catching herself. Conflicting emotions raged inside her. Her body ached to be close to him, to be wrapped in his arms, but her head knew she couldn't allow that.

Tossing his jacket onto his suitcase, he reached for her. "Are okay tonight? You look like you've been crying."

"No." Sara took a step backward putting just enough space between them so he couldn't touch her.

The easy-going smile vanished from Christopher's face. "What's the matter?" Confusion mixed with concern came through his voice.

She'd mentally prepared what she planned to say, but now with him here the words wouldn't come.

"Sara?" He took another step toward her.

The hammering of her heart echoed in her ears. "When we met with David you insisted I do the commercial with you." Okay, not the exact way she planned to start the conversation but it worked.

Christopher stared at her, his forehead scrunched with confusion. "I thought your endorsement would boost support. Before that it looked as if the vote could go either way."

She crossed her arms across her body. "Why did you want it to pass?" She already suspected the answer, but she needed to hear him say it.

"You know why. If the US is going to keep up with the rest of the world, US schools need improvement. Standards need to be higher. There needs to be more emphasis on math and technology." Christopher ran a hand through his hair. "What's this about Sara? You're not making any sense tonight."

"You knew I didn't want my name attached to it, but you insisted anyway. You wanted the contract connected to the plan and knew without the support of my family name the initiative wouldn't pass. You used me to get what you wanted." Anger nearly choked her as the words tumbled from her mouth.

His eyes searched her face for something. "I didn't think my support alone would be enough and I felt the initiative was important—that it could make a real difference, so yeah I tried to change your mind. I don't see how that was using you," he answered sounding defensive.

"Then why didn't you mention the bid?"

Christopher shrugged. "It wasn't my main reason for getting involved. Besides, I didn't think it was a big deal."

"You really expect me to believe that? Do you want to know what I think?" Sara didn't give him the opportunity to answer. "I think you promised David my support before you came to Hawaii and planned on getting me into bed after Jake's wedding," she said, her voice rising with each word. Why couldn't he be honest with her now? His charade was up so it no longer mattered. "What else do you hope to gain by being with me?"

"Where the hell are you getting these ideas?" Christopher's face exploded with color. "If you really believe this crap maybe I should leave now."

Tightening her arms around her, she met his glare. "Yeah, I think you should."

The words hung in the air between them. Christopher's lips parted to speak but then he nodded once, picked up his suitcase, and left.

☙ ❧ ☙

She thinks I used her. How the hell did she come to that conclusion? Christopher balled his shirt up and tossed it on the closet floor. After leaving Sara's townhouse, he drove around for a little while before checking into a hotel. The words from their conversation echoed in his mind. How could she think he'd used her for his personal gain? He'd known the family for years and never once used his association to enhance himself or his company.

Part of him wanted to argue his cause. Make her listen until she admitted she was wrong. The other half insisted he not waste the energy. If she really believed he

would use her and her family then she
didn't know him at all.

Christopher crossed the room to the
minibar. Although not his favorite, he
reached for the bottle of scotch and
poured himself a shot. In one swallow he
tossed down the drink. The alcohol
burned his throat but did nothing to the
anger pulsing inside him. After pouring
another shot he moved to a chair near the
windows. He'd envisioned this weekend
many times over the past few days, but
never had he pictured it going this way.

This time he sipped the drink in his
hand. He'd known that she had trust
issues. She'd told him all about how she'd
overreacted when Callie came into the
picture, but he'd never thought she'd
doubt their relationship. Obviously, he'd
been wrong. How could she think he'd
reached some kind of back room deal with
David Healy? Sure he'd considered the
government contract when he agreed to
support the initiative. It was a logical
move for his company, plain and simple.
She came from a family of business
giants; she must know what a contract
like that meant. But it had never been his
main reason for supporting the initiative.

The phone in his pocket beeped telling
him he'd received a new text message.
Had Sara realized how absurd her ideas

were? Christopher pulled out the phone. Even if she had, then what? Did he just forget about the allegations she'd made?

The four letters glaring back at him from the screen were not the four he hoped to see. *Are we still on for tomorrow?* the message read. Jake, damn it. With the episode at Sara's, he'd forgotten about their plans to have dinner with Charlie and Jake tomorrow night. *Life just keeps getting better.*

A simple no wouldn't suffice. Jake would want to know why and telling him his sister was being stupid wouldn't cut it. Maybe he should tell him to ask Sara for an explanation. Let Jake tell her she was crazy. Jake wouldn't believe for a second that he'd used Sara. Not that it mattered in the long run. His friend had warned him in the beginning about dating his sister, but he hadn't listened. Now he'd probably end up paying the price by losing both his best friend and the woman he loved.

The phone beeped again, a reminder that he hadn't answered the text message. *Change in plans. No go tomorrow,* Christopher wrote.

Why? popped up on the screen.

A new wave of anger rolled through him, this time however, it was directed at him and not Sara. He'd risked his friendship with Jake for his relationship with Sara and it looked like he was about to lose both.

Talk to your sister, Christopher typed before turning off his phone. Let Sara deal with any questions from Jake. Eventually, she'd tell him the whole story anyway.

His jaw clenched just thinking about the story Sara would tell her brother. If any other woman made the same claims against him, Jake would dismiss them outright. Coming from his sister, Jake wouldn't be able to do that. Not that Christopher blamed him. If the tables were reversed he'd have to side with one of his sisters as well. Unfortunately, in this case Sara was dead wrong.

He'd encouraged her to show her support because he believed in the importance of education reform. Even if he hadn't planned on bidding for the government contract, he would have asked her to help him. How could she think any differently? Especially after all the discussions they'd had about education and what America needed to do in order to keep up with the world.

Christopher took another gulp of his scotch. What were the odds she'd come to her senses and realize her mistake? Low to nonexistent. His anger mixed with sadness. They hadn't been together long, but he'd started to think she might be the one. He'd planned to ask her to come to Wisconsin with him and meet his family. No woman he'd ever dated had met his parents.

So much for that plan. Finishing his drink, he contemplated refilling it but passed. The alcohol wasn't doing a thing for him. Anger still flowed through him.

᮫᮫᮫

Sara rolled over in bed. The clock on the nightstand read midnight. She'd been in bed for over an hour yet she remained wide awake. Just like every other night that weekend sleep refused to come. Instead her entire relationship with Christopher played through her head.

Reaching over she grabbed the robe at the foot of her bed. When she had trouble sleeping, she'd lose herself in a book. Tonight her head ached from crying so a book was out, but if she kept the volume low maybe she could pass an hour or so in front of the television with a cup of tea.

The nightlight in the kitchen provided enough illumination and Sara filled the teakettle and set it on the stove. Then she opened the cupboard. Several tins of tea lined the bottom shelf of the cupboard, everything from Earl Grey to Lemon Honey. But one tin stood out from the rest, the Dark Chocolate Mate Tea Christopher had brought her after one of his trips to New York. He told her he'd passed an English tea house and stopped in because it made him think of her. The tea itself wasn't the only gift he'd brought her that weekend. An English bone china tea set accompanied the tea. The night he gave it to her she'd taught him the proper way to make tea using loose leaves rather than tea bags like most Americans used.

She smiled at the memory. Before the lesson he'd insisted tea was tea. No matter how you prepared it, it all tasted the same. After tasting the properly brewed Earl Grey blend, he'd admitted that he'd been wrong. From that day on he frequently had tea when he came to her place rather than his usual coffee.

Whistling filled the silent kitchen and the pleasant memory evaporated into the air much like the steam from the teakettle. Sara grabbed the tin of chamomile tea beside the chocolate mate as her memory moved to their final conversation. He'd looked so mad. She'd never seen him angry before. Not that he had anything to be angry about. He hadn't been the one wronged. No one had stepped all over his heart.

Think about something else. Sara forced herself to focus on each step as she prepared her tea. Then she carried it into the living room, covered herself with a throw blanket, and turned on the television. After a quick scan of the program guide, she settled on reruns of an old nineties sitcom. With any luck it would pass the time and make her laugh.

Chapter 14

What am I supposed to do now? She'd asked herself the same question multiple times over the past two weeks and still had no answer or idea how to figure it out. Entering the kitchen, she turned on the stove. Even though it was Friday evening, she was still at home. In fact these days she hardly left her townhouse. Instead she stayed safely hidden away from everyone. And while it was a self-imposed confinement, she hadn't adjusted to it. Since joining David Healy's campaign she'd eaten, slept, and breathed politics. Now that her political career and Christopher were gone, gaping voids were left in her life.

Leaving her position as David's chief of staff had been one of the most difficult things she'd ever done, yet she'd had no choice. As much as she loved working on the Hill, she couldn't continue working for David after the way he manipulated her. Which brought her back to her unanswered question—what was she supposed to do now?

Maybe if she got some sleep she could sort her future out, but sleep refused to come, despite the absolute exhaustion plaguing her body. Instead her thoughts constantly returned to Christopher. They hadn't spoken since the evening she confronted him in her townhouse. He hadn't called or texted, and neither had she.

Right after their argument she'd expected him to call and try to convince her she was wrong. As the days passed and he didn't call she realized that he didn't intend to. In her book that only further proved his guilt. If he hadn't used her wouldn't he defend himself? His lack of effort meant either he was guilty or just didn't care.

Either way it was over between them. Her head knew it, now if she could only get her heart on the same page, maybe her world would return to normal, or something close to normal. But how does someone do that, Sara wondered getting up to make her tea?

She couldn't throw herself into her work anymore. What else did she have?

Maybe the key was to get out more, even if only to see family. She'd canceled plans with Jake twice, both times via text message. It'd been easier that way. Over the phone he would know something was wrong and drag it out of her. In fact she hadn't spoken to him once since the breakup. With a text message she could tell him she didn't feel well and he wouldn't know the difference. At least that worked for now. Eventually, he would get suspicious and start asking questions and she'd have to tell him everything. The thought of it made her sick to her stomach. She always fell into the same trap with men. Although she'd never tell Jake the real reason their relationship ended; it was possible that Christopher had already told her brother about the breakup. A brief jolt of sympathy shot through her. When Jake found out Christopher manipulated her, it would end their friendship.

"It's not my fault if it does." Sara carried her tea into her bedroom and flicked on the lamp. The soft light bounced off the pale pink walls casting a warm glow. "He should have thought of that before." The guilt remained, gnawing at her insides despite her words. Even if his actions had led to the end of their relationship, perhaps she should have thought harder about how their involvement would affect Jake. At the time she'd put very little thought into it at all. Had Christopher?

Slipping into her favorite pajamas, she grabbed her book. Time with a good novel and a hot cup of tea might help distract her and push all thoughts of Jake and Christopher from her mind for a bit. When the doorbell chimed, Sara froze in place, her heart beating fast. No one came by without calling her first, not even her mother.

Tossing her book down, Sara pressed the button under the security screen near her bed. The console gave her access to the video monitor posted outside her front door. She almost expected to see Christopher there, but instead she found Jake standing on the front steps. With a groan she released the breath she'd been holding. What did he want? Had he realized she'd gone out of her way to avoid him? She'd known it would happen at some point, but hoped it'd take him a bit more time.

Maybe if I take my time answering the door he'll go away. No sooner did the thought pass through her head and the doorbell rang again. Evidently, her brother planned to be stubborn tonight. "The sooner I answer, the sooner he'll leave me in peace," she said as she walked to the door.

"Took you long onough," Jako ooid rather than give her a proper greeting when she opened the door.

"I was getting changed," she answered.

He gave her a once-over before his eyes settled back on her face. "You look like hell. Are you sick?" He walked into the living room and sat on the love seat without being invited inside.

"Thanks, you really know how to make me feel good." Someone needed to remind her brother of the old saying: if you don't have anything good to say, don't say anything at all.

Jake propped his feet on the coffee table. "Well you do. Are you feeling okay?" True brotherly concern filled his voice this time.

"I'm fine. Just busy." Sara perched herself on the edge of the chair next to him.

"Then what's with canceling dinner and not returning my calls?"

Before he'd walked through the door, her brother had known the status of her health. He'd been trying to catch her in a lie and succeeded. She knew his ways well and should have picked her words more carefully.

"Like I said, I'm busy. You're not the only one with responsibilities," she answered. Her defenses automatically went into play.

"Never said you didn't, but something is up. Both you and Christopher are avoiding me like the plague. So what gives?"

"We haven't talked in weeks. You'll have to ask him what his problem is."

Jake's feet hit the floor and he straightened up. "What happened?" he asked, his voice turning cold.

Sara looked down at her hands folded in her lap. Should she keep the answer short and sweet or give him all the details. The less information she gave, the less a fool she'd look for letting a man use her again. "I ended things. It just wasn't working." Omitting the truth wouldn't hurt anyone.

Jake's eyebrow went up and he gave her a look that said bullshit. "Not buying it, sis. What happened?"

"It's not important. Let it go." Jake's insistence on knowing the details irked her. She'd never nosed around his relationships.

"Any other time fine, but not now." Jake crossed his arms across his chest.

She envisioned herself tossing the crystal vase of flowers at her brother's head. Whatever happened with Christopher wasn't any of his business. But she knew he'd stick around until she gave him some details.

"You heard that the education initiative passed right? Did you know that Hall Technology was awarded the government contract associated with it?" Sara asked with as reasonable a voice as she could manage, considering the jumble of emotions simmering inside.

Jake shrugged one shoulder. "I didn't know, but it makes sense that Christopher would go for the contract."

"Have you noticed that the value of Hall Technology's stock spiked?" Sara watched his face for any reaction to her words.

"I own stock in the company, of course I noticed. But what does that have to do with you and him?"

Evidently she needed to spell it out for him. "All of that is because of me. Both he and David used me to get what they wanted. There wouldn't even be a contract, if I hadn't attached the Sherbrooke name to the education initiative. And his stocks only spiked after the company got the contract."

"Have you been putting something besides sugar in your tea, Sara?" he asked leaning toward her, confusion in his eyes.

"Christopher wouldn't use you like that. That's not the kind of guy he is."

Sara held back a snort. How dare he defend Christopher? "Why else would he have urged me to support the education plan? He knew the likelihood of getting it through the Senate was slim without the Sherbrooke name attached. And what else could've caused such a spike in stock value if not the announcement that Hall Technology won the contract? I don't believe for a second it was all a coincidence."

Jake gave her a look of pity. "The stock started to go up around the time Hall Technology announced its plan to buy a Japanese technology company. No matter what you think, he never would have asked for your public support of the initiative because he wanted the government contract. He would've supported that type of thing even if no monetary gain was involved."

She'd expected Jake to be angry with Christopher, not defend him. "Believe what you want, Jake. It doesn't matter anyway." If he wanted to side with Christopher, she wasn't going to make a big deal about it.

Jake reached for her tightly balled-up hand. "Phillip would've done those things.

Not Christopher," he said his voice gentle and understanding.

"You have your opinion and I have mine." Up until two weeks ago, she would've agreed with her brother but not anymore. While Christopher wasn't trying to ruin her father by using her like Phillip, he still ranked up there on her list of jerks.

"Come on, Sara. You really believe he'd use you in any way to help his company? Don't you think he would've tried something before now? I mean I've known him for years and he's never pulled anything like that with me."

Her brother's tone of voice told her exactly what he thought of her assumptions, but just because he didn't agree with her, didn't mean she was wrong. "Please let it go, Jake. It doesn't matter anyway." Sara rubbed her temple with her hand. The headache she'd fought all day was back.

"Sure. You look like you don't care," Jake answered sarcastically giving her the once-over.

If she asked him to leave what were the chances he would go? Knowing Jake, not very high. He tended to do things his way. Most days she loved that about him. Not today though. "I know he's your friend but butt out Jake." Sara let her annoyance seep into her voice. "When you were on the outs with Charlie, I didn't give you advice."

Jake threw up his hands. "Whatever. If you want to act like an idiot go ahead. When you're ready to talk you know where I am."

The silver Mercedes parked next to his sister's car reminded Christopher of their conversation that morning. Caroline told him William was coming for dinner and she'd like him to join them. With everything else on his mind, he'd forgotten all about it. If he'd remembered he wouldn't have come straight home. In his current mood—one he feared was becoming permanent—he'd make a lousy dinner companion.

Since his breakup with Sara, he'd been like an enraged bull in mourning. Or at least that was how Caroline described him, and he thought it was a good comparison.

Christopher remained in his car weighing his options. If he went inside, he could easily avoid his sister and her dinner guest the house was big enough. He disliked the idea of going inside and then intentionally avoiding his sister though. He knew she wanted him to meet William. He'd always been the first family member Caroline introduced to a new boyfriend. If he didn't like the guy, Caroline usually ended things with him soon after. Normally, he didn't mind the ritual. Tonight though the idea of assessing his sister's newest love ranked right up there with going to the dentist.

Dealing with the club scene on Friday nights held about as much interest. Before his relationship with Sara he'd stopped in some of the exclusive nightclubs once or twice a month—more for something to do than the love of it. It had been a while since his last visit, and he found he had no desire to go back. A drive held some appeal, but the rain ruled that out for him. If he had to worry about hydroplaning on slick roads he wouldn't enjoy it.

I might as well go inside. Resigned, Christopher climbed out of the car. Perhaps a quick hello would be enough and then he could retire upstairs, grab a beer, and turn on a movie. He could sit down with his sister and her new boyfriend some other night.

What he intended to be a short introduction turned into a twenty-minute conversation. Christopher suspected it would've been even longer if he'd allowed it. Now up in the privacy of his suite, he randomly flipped through his movie collection. So far he'd gone through at least one hundred movies, yet none of them interested him. After looking through the sci-fi collection, he scrolled over to the classics and Casablanca showed up as the first movie in his list.

Hell. He should have skipped the category altogether. Seeing all the classics they'd watched together only reminded him of Sara, especially Casablanca. It'd been the first of many they'd watched, and he didn't need any reminders of her. Even without them, she popped into his head throughout the day.

Christopher scanned through the collection of action movies, but his mind remained on Sara. He thought she'd come to her senses and call him, but the more time that passed the less likely it seemed. As much as he wanted to hear her voice, a call to her was out. While he may still want her, he wasn't going to beg, especially when he had done nothing wrong. She'd been the one to jump to some absurd conclusions, not him.

While the opening scene of the first Terminator film played out on the screen, the last time he saw Sara played out in his head. When she started accusing him, his temper flared and not long after that he walked out. Should he have stayed and

THE BILLIONAIRE PRINCESS   271

tried harder to convince her? Would it have made a difference?

Probably not. At the time she hadn't been thinking with her head.

The way things stood now, he figured she either still believed her crazy ideas about him or had come to her senses but didn't care enough to work things out. Their conversation when they woke up in bed together in Hawaii reverberated in his mind. She commented how they were both adults and how often she'd slept with men while campaigning with the senator. Maybe he'd been just another guy in her long line of men. Perhaps he'd assumed the relationship meant more to her than it did.

Whatever the truth, he needed to move on and put their relationship and perhaps his friendship with Jake behind him. So far he'd avoided texts from Jake. Although he never referred to Sara, Christopher assumed Jake now knew they were no longer together. Avoiding Jake may be the coward's way out, but he found it a better option. The alternative could lead to a very ugly situation.

Christopher ended up watching two more movies before calling it a night. He wanted to drift off into a dreamless sleep, but that never came. Finally after tossing and turning for hours Christopher gave up falling asleep and headed out for a drive. With no specific location in mind, he drove around for two hours before returning home feeling no more relaxed than when he left. The scent of freshly cooked bacon and cinnamon greeted him when he entered the gourmet kitchen.

"You're up early," he said to Caroline who sat on a stool at the island.

"William and I have plans for the day. He should be here in about an hour. Where have you been?" she asked, looking over his outfit.

Christopher poured himself a cup of coffee and took a sip of the strong French roast before answering. "Out for a drive."

Caroline frowned, her expression reminding him of their mother. With her wavy golden brown hair, dark brown eyes, and fair complexion, she looked like a younger version of Gail Hall. "Thinking about Sara again?"

To say he was thinking about her again gave the impression he'd stopped which he never had. He would never admit that, so instead he shrugged. "Didn't William spend the night?"

"This isn't my house, so I didn't ask him. If you would have stuck around last night you'd know that," Caroline answered sounding hurt.

Christopher snatched a slice of bacon off his sister's plate. "Trust me, you didn't want me around last night. I would've made lousy company."

"How's that any different than usual lately?" she asked with a fair amount of sarcasm. "What happened between you two anyway?"

He took another sip of coffee and debated how best to answer without going into details. "It just didn't work between us."

"Then I suggest you forget about her and move on for everyone's sake. Especially yours. You've been miserable for weeks."

He never meant to take his unhappiness out on anyone else.

"If you want to talk or anything, I'm here Christopher." Caroline took the final sip of her juice and then put her dishes in the dishwasher.

How many times in the past had his sisters come to him when one of their relationships ended? More times than he could count, especially Caroline. With only eighteen months between them, they'd always been especially close. Yet it'd never occurred to him to seek her out for help. "Thanks, I'll keep that in mind."

Caroline walked over and hugged him. "I need to finish getting ready. I'll see you later."

Long after Caroline left he remained, mulling over her words. This was the first time she'd called him out for his foul mood. Somehow he needed to move on and put everything with Sara in the past. His foul mood wasn't changing anything. The only thing it accomplished was offending others. His sister was right; he needed to forget about Sara Sherbrooke.

Often when he started a new project, it took over his life, blocking out everything else until he completed it. Perhaps that was just the thing he needed now. A new project to sink his teeth into. Something to keep his body and mind engaged.

Christopher grabbed an apple from the fruit basket on the counter and headed for his office. On his computer he kept a file of new ideas he thought he could develop at some point, and from where he now stood, some point had arrived.

Chapter 15

The heavy traffic between her parents' apartment on West 72nd Street and Dylan's penthouse made her grateful she had taken the limo. She could use the time on her laptop rather than stuck behind the wheel of a car. Unfortunately, the traffic also gave her time to reassess her decision. Back home talking to Callie about her relationship problems seemed like a good idea. Callie knew Christopher but wasn't emotionally invested in the situation like Jake. She already knew about Sara's past disastrous relationship with Phillip, so she wouldn't need to share that with anyone else, and she'd had her own rocky road with her husband before getting married.

Now Sara's confidence in her decision waned. For all intents and purposes, Callie and she remained strangers. They only knew the most basic of information about each other. Even though they'd agreed to start over, so far they hadn't spent any time getting to know each other.

Despite her misgivings, Sara kept silent, not asking the driver to take her back to her parents' apartment. Something deep inside told her to follow through with her decision. Not once during their previous conversation had Callie exhibited anything but grace and understanding. Right now she needed advice and someone that understood.

Sara stepped off the elevator and paused in front of Callie and Dylan's door. She hadn't visited in a while but from out here everything looked unchanged. *The worst that can happen is I leave here feeling as miserable and confused as I do now. It can't get much worse.* Sara moved toward the doorbell but before she could press it the door swung open.

"Sara." Dylan stopped dead in his tracks, his hand still on the doorknob. "Is something wrong? I'm on my way back to the office but if you need—" Dressed in a dark blue suit with a red tie, her half-brother could have been the poster boy for corporate America if it wasn't for his expression. Concern and confusion filled his face.

"Everything is fine. I... uh... wanted to talk to Callie."

Dylan's jaw dropped and with difficulty she stopped herself from laughing at his expression. She'd never seen her brother so shell-shocked in her life. She wished she had a camera to capture his expression.

"You came to talk with Callie?" Dylan asked slowly.

Sara nodded somewhat enjoying her brother's shock. "That's okay right? She is my sister."

"Of course." Dylan pushed the door fully open again. "She's in the media room with Lauren. I'll walk you in before I leave."

Sara followed her brother through the main living room. At one time the room contained nothing but black leather furniture and lots of glass—a room devoid of character. Now warm colors softened the room and pictures hung on the walls making it feel more like a home than a cold sterile apartment. The scent of something chocolaty added to the homey feeling. A little bit of envy shot through her. She'd never begrudge her half-brother happiness, but for a split-second jealousy reared its head. It seemed he'd found his soul mate, while all she'd managed to find so far was heartbreak and jerks.

Reaching out she laid her hand on his arm to stop him. When he looked over at her she blurted out the words she wanted to say before she could change her mind. "I know I never told you, but I'm really happy for you."

Dylan's eyebrows shot up. "Uh, thank you." The tone of his voice indicated he wanted to say more, but he kept it to himself.

Through the open door, Sara heard Callie and Laura McDonald talking in the media room. The two women had been friends for years and seemed extremely close.

"Callie, Sara's here to see you," Dylan called into the room from the doorway.

Silence filled the room and two sets of eyes focused on her. *Yep should've called first.*

"I can come back later if you want," Sara said, almost hoping Callie would agree. Talking about her relationship problems with Callie was one thing, but she didn't want to do it with Lauren around too.

Callie and Lauren exchanged a quick look, "I'll take Lucky for a walk. I need to burn off the brownies Callie made anyway." Lauren stood.

"We can take the elevator down together," Dylan said, standing in the doorway.

Callie waited until her husband and friend left before speaking. "Please sit down. Are you hungry? I made some double chocolate chip brownies."

The sweet smell of chocolate she'd noticed when she came in teased her senses making Callie's offer tempting. Unfortunately the ball of nerves in her stomach suggested that eating was a bad idea. "Maybe later, thanks." Sara took a seat across from Callie.

Silence fell between them. Sara didn't know exactly how to begin. Thankfully she didn't have to. "Are you staying in the city long?" Callie asked.

"Until tomorrow. I only came... well... to see you actually." Sara picked her words as she went along. "I needed someone to talk to."

Callie nibbled on her bottom lip, a clear sign of her discomfort. "And you picked me?" Disbelief colored her words.

Sara felt heat flood her face. "I don't have many close friends and none that know about what happened with Phillip." Swallowing, she fought to control her swirling emotions.

"I'm guessing this involves Christopher."

With a nod Sara launched into the entire story including her conversation with Jake during his unexpected visit to her place. Not once did Callie interrupt her or give any indication of her thoughts.

"Sara, I'm not sure what you want me to say," Callie said when Sara finished the entire story.

Sara tugged the end of her ponytail, twisting several strands around her finger. "Your opinion, I guess. One minute I know I made the right call, the next I'm wondering if I jumped to conclusions. I keep going back and forth. Jake's no help, he and Christopher have been friends for too long."

"Jake does know him better than I do," Callie said gently.

"That's the problem. I need a neutral opinion, Callie. Please. Do you think I'm wrong?" She needed someone's help sorting out her mixed feelings.

Callie didn't speak at first. "I understand why you reacted the way you did. It sounds like Phillip was a real ass," Callie paused. "Before all this did you ever once think Christopher was the type to use his connection to the family?"

Sara didn't pause before answering. "No. He rarely mentioned his association with the family."

"And who made the first move, him or you?"

Sara thought about the night in Hawaii after Jake's wedding and then about their time in Los Angeles. "Neither really. It just happened." Sara released the hair twisted around her finger. "You think I'm wrong don't you?"

Callie leaned closer. "It doesn't matter what I think or anyone else. Your opinion is the one that matters. What does your heart say?"

A tear rolled down her cheek. "I want to be wrong. But—"

"But what, Sara? Has he given you any reason not to trust him?"

"No," she spoke the word without hesitation. Before she'd heard Miriam Walker on CZN, she never doubted his motives for being with her. "Still that—"

"Sara, you need to do whatever feels right. But I think you're wrong about Christopher." Callie looked her directly in the eye. "And if you don't start trusting people soon you're going to end up alone. You'll always find some way to doubt someone's true intentions. Do you really want to live like that?"

Callie's words stung. The picture Callie painted was bleak, but she recognized the truth in her half-sister's words.

"You don't know what it's like to be used by someone because of who you are. To have people cozy up to you because your last name is Sherbrooke." Bitterness crept into her voice.

"You don't know why I ended things with Dylan that summer, do you?"

Sara shook her head. She remembered their relationship came to a sudden end sometime after a big fundraiser in New York City, but she'd never learned the specifics. Since they eventually worked out their differences and married she'd never asked.

Over the next few minutes Callie explained how she'd overheard Marty Phillips, their father's campaign manager at the time, tell Dylan that he'd been the perfect man to keep her occupied and away from the media until Warren made his announcement about who she was. Sara's heart ached as Callie told her how she'd rushed out of the Waldorf Astoria and caught a train back to Massachusetts. And she understood why Callie refused to listen when Dylan followed her; although she secretly thought his drive from New York to Massachusetts that night in the pouring rain was romantic.

"I can't believe Dylan agreed to that. And you forgave him completely?" Put in a similar position, she didn't think should be as forgiving.

"I guess love lets you do things that you don't think you could ever do." Callie gave her a small smile. "If you love Christopher as much as I think you do, then—"

"I should reconsider things?" Sara said interrupting her.

Callie shrugged. "Either that or talk to him. Give him a chance to explain his side. It sounds like he deserves at least that much."

Sara left Callie almost as conflicted as when she arrived. She'd hoped that talking about the situation with a neutral party would somehow make it clearer, but even after the heart-to-heart it remained cloudy. Regardless, she didn't regret her visit. Callie's comments forced her to take a step back and view their entire relationship from the outside. Despite everything Jake had said during their conversation, she hadn't been able to look beyond her own perceptions.

Now back at her parents' apartment, Sara scrutinized every aspect of her time with Christopher, starting with Jake's wedding. Heat blossomed in her body and spread outward as memories of that night returned. It been spontaneous and so unlike her. Yet at the same time it felt natural, like they belonged together, until the next morning when embarrassment and guilt set in. If he'd agreed to some back-room deal with David Healy would he have avoided her afterward? Wouldn't he have tried right then and there to start something permanent with her?

Several weeks had passed before she saw him again at the fundraiser in Providence. That night he'd told her upfront that David invited him. He hadn't given her some line about being there just to see her, which would've been a great way to show his interest.

Sara twisted a strand of hair around her finger. So far nothing from her memories pointed toward some grand scheme between Christopher and the senator. Their trip to California however, had been Christopher's idea entirely. He'd convinced her to publicly support the plan and make the commercial with him.

Sara pushed everything about the trip from her mind, except that first night in her hotel room. He hadn't pushed her that night. When she backed off and insisted they stop, he respected her decision. Even now she remembered the gratitude she'd felt toward him for being so understanding. A man with an ulterior motive wouldn't act like that, would he? Her ex had pursued her like a dog in heat. Even now after all that had happened between them, Phillip tried to lure her back from time to time.

The longer she sat examining their relationship the clearer the truth became, she'd been wrong. Once again she'd let her fears and mistrust ruin a relationship. Anger and disgust toward herself boiled up inside making it hard to breathe. With her hand she wiped away the tears that rolled down her cheeks. How could she have been so stupid yet again? She'd been too trusting with Phillip and too distrusting with first Callie and now Christopher. When would she learn? Sara's tears turned to gut-wrenching sobs as the enormity of what she'd lost set in.

Hours later Sara stared at the ceiling wide-awake. Her head throbbed and her eyes burned from her emotional breakdown. Despite her physical discomforts and exhaustion her brain refused to rest. Instead questions ran through her head. Should she attempt an apology? Was it possible for them to pick up where they'd left off? Could she handle it if she made the first move and he rejected her? She needed answers. Unfortunately, she didn't have a single one and the only way to answer them involved further heartache. Something she didn't know if she could handle right now.

His office door slammed closed with so much force the painting on the wall shook. Immediately, Christopher spun his chair around and came to his feet. He wasn't expecting any visitors and his sister wouldn't slam the door with such force.

"What the hell is wrong with you, Hall?" Jake moved toward Christopher's desk, his jaw clenched tightly. "First you make my sister miserable, then you blow me off." Jake walked around the desk and stopped when they were only a foot apart.

Christopher almost wanted to laugh. He'd made Sara miserable? More like it was the other way around. She'd been the one making the accusations. "I don't think you got the whole story. She told me to leave."

Jake crossed his arms across his chest. "I know all about that. But you haven't even tried to talk to her."

Why should he bother? If she could think he'd used her for his own gains, she didn't trust him at all. How could they have a relationship if she didn't trust him? "It's none of your business, Jake."

"When my sister is miserable and heartbroken because of you, it becomes my business." Jake took a step closer.

"Heartbroken?" Christopher laughed bitterly at the absurd idea. "She'll move on in no time. She admitted to me after your wedding that going from guy to guy is normal for her."

Since the breakup he'd forced himself not to picture her with another man. Now that he mentioned it though, the image filled his mind. His hands balled up into fists as he pictured her lying next to some Washington politician, her silky blonde hair draped across a pillow as she slept.

"She told you what? And you believed her?"

Perhaps her exact words that morning in Hawaii had been more like things like this happen all the time but they were arguing semantics. "Something along those lines."

"She lied to you. You're the first guy she's been with since Phillip Young."

Phillip Young, the name sounded familiar. Christopher searched his memory.

"She broke up with him a few years ago when she learned he started their relationship to dig up dirt on our father during the campaign."

A light bulb went on inside his head. Phillip was the guy giving her a hard time at the fundraiser. He looked like the blackmailing type. "Okay, fine. She doesn't sleep around. That doesn't change a thing. If she wants to talk, she knows how to contact me. And just for the record I didn't use our relationship to get that contract."

"You have no idea the number Phillip did on her." Jake ran a hand through his hair. "She hasn't been herself since. She was finally getting back to normal with you."

The anger he felt toward Jake for calling him out like this shifted to Phillip. The night he'd met him at the fundraiser he wanted to punch him because of the hard time he gave Sara. Now with this new knowledge he longed for the opportunity to do much worse. "I get it Jake, but that doesn't change the facts. She told me to leave." The final conversation was etched in his mind, right down to the expression on her face and the way she stood.

Jake took a step closer, his face a mask of controlled anger. "You're being an ass, you know that?"

Christopher teetered between telling Jake off and punching him in the face. Either move would be bad for their friendship. Instinctively, his hand formed a fist again. "I think you should leave, Sherbrooke." Christopher spoke through clenched teeth.

Jake narrowed his eyes as his jaw worked overtime grinding his teeth to dust. "Whatever. It's your loss."

Before Christopher could respond, Jake marched out of the room and slammed the door behind him. *Dammit.* What a mess he created. Christopher dropped back down into his chair and swirled around so he faced the window overlooking the garden. How much of what Jake said could he believe? Usually he'd say every word, but not this time. Sara's lack of trust in him cut deep even now, weeks after their argument. No matter how he felt, if any chance of them getting back together existed, she would have to make the first move. He'd attempted to argue his side that night and she refused to listen. He wasn't going to confront her again just so she could make more absurd accusations. Who in their right mind would want to set themselves up for that type of treatment?

Long after the sun disappeared from the sky, Christopher remained looking out the window with a tiny seed of an idea in his head. While he would not confront her again and beg her to take

him   back,   maybe   he
could   prove   to   her   that   he   hadn't
manipulated her into a relationship for
his own benefit.

Chapter 16

For the second time that week she had broken down in tears. Earlier that week Callie called asking if she wanted to talk anymore about her relationship problems. Almost immediately tears started falling, not as much in reaction to Callie's question as to Callie's thoughtfulness. The more she got to know her half-sister, the worse she felt about the way she treated her in the beginning.

This time her waterworks were set off by a picture on the cover of Today magazine. The picture showed Christopher and her together the night of her mom's birthday bash. The headline beneath it read "No Happily Ever After For This Sherbrooke."

"I think it's a great picture of you at least," Hannah said. She still held the magazine she brought with her when she stopped by to return a few things Sara had left behind at her office. "The article says you broke up with him after you found him in bed with another woman. Is that true?"

Sara bit down on her lip and wiped a tear away with a tissue. The media printed whatever got the most sales. "No Hannah, you can't believe everything you read. Remember that." She'd told the younger woman that on countless occasions, yet it still failed to sink in.

"I'm glad. He seems like a nice guy. Did you hear about what he did?

Sara shook her head.

"He established a new grant program for elementary schools. It's similar to the Reading First Grant currently in place but rather than provide money for reading intervention it will focus on math. He's urging other large corporations to contribute. So far two more are on board.

The words slowly sunk in. She'd already reached the conclusion she'd been wrong about Christopher but this latest news really drove it home. Sara pushed back her chair. She needed a few minutes to regroup. "I'll be back."

Turning on the bathroom sink, Sara splashed cold water on her face. She couldn't go on like this much longer. Either she needed to bury her feelings or confront Christopher and attempt to salvage their relationship. "You've become a chicken," she said to the reflection gazing back at her in the mirror. "How did you let that happen?" The how didn't matter. Getting past it did.

Sara reapplied her mascara. What had Callie said to her about love? It lets you do things you never thought you could do. Maybe Callie was right. Straightening her back, Sara stared at her reflection and finally made her decision. She'd make the first move. A wave of nausea rolled through her as she thought about confronting Christopher. Even with it her confidence in the decision grew. She couldn't spend her life wondering what if. She needed closure one way or the other.

"Hannah, thank you for bringing my things by. I appreciate it," Sara gripped the back of a kitchen chair. "Let's get together soon."

Once alone Sara reached for her phone, but held back from dialing. *It's the right thing.*

Hitting the contact icon on her phone, she scrolled through the list of names until she came to Caroline, Christopher's executive assistant. Before she hopped a plane and flew to California she needed to make sure he was around.

"I'm not at liberty to discuss Mr. Hall's schedule," Caroline answered after Sara asked about his plans.

Sara knew this was a standard practice, but in the past Caroline had been forthcoming with such information. Obviously their breakup caused her to have a change of heart. "Please Caroline. I have to talk to him and I can't do that on the phone. I need to see him."

"It's against—"

"I know all about company policy. But please, I want to set things right between us, Caroline," Sara pleaded, infusing all her emotions into her voice.

Caroline remained silent for what seemed like an eternity. "He'll be home tonight. Tomorrow he's attending the Literacy Across America Charity event and Sunday afternoon he's playing golf with Congressman Stuart," Caroline answered with reluctance.

It didn't give her much time, but she'd take what she could get. "I'll be there tonight. Please don't tell him." She waited, unsure whether or not Caroline would agree.

"Okay."

"One battle down," Sara said after ending her conversation. Now all that remained was convincing Christopher to forgive her.

Sara swallowed the bile rising in her throat as the wheels of the jet touched down. Releasing her death grip on the arms of her seat, she stood and took a few deep calming breaths. For once it wasn't her fear of flying making her a nervous wreck, but her fear of confronting Christopher that had her nerves working on overdrive.

"Right to your hotel, Ms. Sherbrooke?" the limo driver asked when she stepped off the plane.

"No. I need to stop at this address first."

With a simple nod the driver accepted the paper as he held Sara's door open for her. Once she was inside, he closed the door and got behind the steering wheel.

I can do this. Sara wiped her sweaty palms against her jeans. She'd chosen to dress casually today in jeans and a dark purple top. She'd even opted for a simple ponytail and just lip gloss. On several occasions Christopher commented how much he liked it when she dressed in jeans and skipped the heavier makeup. Would he notice that she'd dressed with him in mind? Or would he be so annoyed at seeing her after all this time that her efforts went unnoticed? Only one way to find out.

When the car pulled up to the security gate at Christopher's house, she held her breath for half a minute. Carolyn had promised to alert security prior to Sara's arrival, but she feared Christopher's sister might have had a change of heart. But like so many times before, security opened the gate leading up to Christopher's property.

"Christopher went straight to his office when he came home," Caroline informed her when she greeted Sara in the main foyer. "I'm just warning you he looked miserable, so don't be surprised if he's in a bad mood."

Sara sighed inwardly. Convincing him to give them another chance might be difficult, but with him in a bad mood the task may be next to impossible.

"You know where his office is, right?"

"Yes." Sara took a step then stopped. "Thank you for your help, Caroline."

Caroline held her gaze for a moment. Sara sensed the woman wanted to say something but nothing ever came. Instead she nodded and headed off toward another part of the house.

Blood pounded in her ears as she followed the marble hallway toward Christopher's office. On the plane she'd rehearsed several apologies, but none sounded quite right so she'd have to wing it now. Assuming of course he didn't ask her to leave the minute she walked in. Stopping in front of the door, Sara readjusted her ponytail, wiped her sweaty hands on her jeans, and knocked.

"I told you Caroline, I don't want to talk," Christopher's voice called through the door.

The sound of his voice brought tears to her eyes. Blinking them away, she turned the doorknob and entered without saying a word. At first she remained silent. Her eyes soaked up the sight of him after so many weeks apart. Seated behind a sleek ebony desk, he faced his computer screen. He'd rolled up the sleeves of his light blue dress shirt and a tie hung over the back of his chair. From the doorway she could only see his profile, but his voice told her plenty about his current mood.

"Caroline, if you came in here to..." Christopher's voice trailed off when he turned and discovered her standing there. In the blink of an eye his expression changed from annoyance to confusion. "Sara, I thought... What are you doing here?" Christopher stood but remained behind his desk.

Being so close yet unable to touch him made her heart ache. More than anything she wanted to press her body against his, wrap her arms around him, and tell him how much he meant to her. Thanks to her insecurities, she'd lost that right. If she was lucky though, she would earn it back. Sara took a tentative step forward, her hands clasped behind her back. "I came to talk to you." All the rehearsed speeches went straight out of her head. "All you need to do is listen, okay?" Sara closed the gap between her and the desk, her fingernails biting into her hands behind her back.

Nodding, Christopher sat back down, the expression on his face changing to curiosity.

"Before you, my last relationship was with Phillip Young. You met him at the fundraiser in Providence."

"I remember he was giving you a hard time that night." Christopher's eyes met hers and for a moment she felt like he could see her every thought.

"We met right before my father received the party's nomination for president. Things got serious very fast. I actually thought he might propose. Anyway about eight months before the election, I learned the truth about Phillip. He worked for Governor Richardson. His goal was to dig up anything to use against my father. I don't know if Richardson hired him directly or if someone in Richardson's camp hired him, but it meant the same thing. He had no real interest in me. He was using me to get close to the family."

Sara paused. Talking about the past and how gullible she'd been brought on a rush of anger. "Around the time that relationship ended, my father learned about Callie. For a long time I didn't trust her. I figured she must want something too."

"You've known me for a long time, Sara. How could—"

She knew what he was about to say. "I didn't at first. Then I saw Miriam Walker on The Brown Report and the things she said had me thinking. Everything sort of went downhill after that." Sara shifted her weight from one foot to the other. So far he'd given no indication how he felt about her and her explanation. "I admit, when I get emotional I'm not the most logical person."

"When we were together, it was always about us. I'd never do anything to hurt you." The affection in his voice sent hope through her heart.

"I know, and I'm sorry. If I could go back and change the things I said that night I would." Sara choked.

Christopher stood and came around the front of his desk. "Since you can't change the past, where does that leave us now?"

Sara fought to hold back a smile. He hadn't agreed to anything yet. "I hope we can go back to the way we were before I screwed up." She moved closer to him. "I've missed you so much," she said softly reaching for his hand.

With one sharp tug, he pulled her against him, his body solid and warm next to hers. Burying her face against his shoulder, she took a deep breath, inhaling the combination of his cologne and soap. "I love you. I'm so sorry I hurt you." Sara managed to get the words out around the lump in her throat.

"I love you too." With his lips pressed against the top of her head, the words were a little muffled but she could easily understand them.

Christopher feared his chest might burst with happiness. Not only was Sara in his arms again, but she'd told him she loved him. He tilted her face toward his and kissed her, keeping the kiss gentle and short. If he gave in to the desire surging through his body now, he'd never say what he needed to.

Bringing the kiss to an end, he pulled back to look at her, his arms still wrapped around her waist. "Before we move forward, I need you to promise me something. The next time anything bothers you talk to me, okay? No matter what it is. Even if you think I'll consider it ridiculous, talk to me." Christopher paused giving his words a chance to sink in. I don't want something like this happening again between us."

Sara's tear-filled eyes looked back at him and his throat tightened with emotion.

"I can do that," she said.

Satisfied with her answer, he captured her lips for another kiss. This one was more urgent and demanding as he allowed all his pent-up emotions free reign. Digging his hands into her hair, he used his mouth to show how much he'd missed her.

"Maybe we should continue this reunion upstairs," she said. Sara pulled back when his hands slipped under the hem of her shirt and settled on her back.

Christopher kissed her again. "I like the way you think." With lightning speed he grabbed her hand and tugged her out of the room toward the staircase.

◌◌◌

Christopher propped himself up on one elbow and studied the woman sleeping next to him. When he first woke up he thought he dreamed it all, but here she was sound asleep in his bed. Even with the proof next to him, it seemed like a dream. When he turned around in his office earlier that evening and saw her standing there, he feared for a second he'd started imagining things. Dressed so casually in jeans and no makeup, she'd looked the way she did in his dreams.

Reaching out he ran his fingers down her arm. Her skin was warm and solid. Definitely not an image his mind conjured up. Yet even with all the evidence pointing toward the truth, it almost seemed too good to be true. He not only had Sara back, but she loved him. She'd told him that more than once since she walked into in his office hours earlier. Unable to stop himself, he leaned down and kissed her. Slowly Sara's eyes fluttered open and she smiled at him.

"Hey," she said, her voice still groggy with sleep.

"Hey yourself," he said joining their hands.

"For a second there I thought I was dreaming." Sara brought their joined hands toward her lips and kissed his hand.

"Trust me, we're both wide awake, sweetheart."

Epilogue

Sara dumped her bag on the floor next to the full-sized bed pushed against the wall. She could picture Christopher growing up in this room, sitting at the desk near the window studying or playing on the braided rug in the middle of the room. Unzipping her bag, she began to unpack while waiting for Christopher to come up. When she'd left the kitchen, he'd still been deep in conversation with his mom about the preparations for his sister's birthday party. He wanted to have it catered, but his mom insisted on preparing all the food. After seeing their disagreement, Sara knew where his stubbornness came from.

Since getting back together four months earlier, she'd seen that side of him on numerous occasions. Not that she was complaining. After all, she had a stubborn streak of her own, a fact that occasionally caused them to butt heads. In the end though they always managed to reach some kind of compromise no matter the issue.

In search of some clothes hangers Sara walked to the closet door and pulled it open. A few long-sleeved shirts and a winter jacket hung in the closet, items she guessed Christopher left when visiting his parents. The shelf above the clothing rod was stacked high with old board games and science kits as well as models of space shuttles and science fair trophies. From the looks of it Gail Hall had held on to many mementos from Christopher's past.

Careful not to knock anything down, she reached up and lifted one of the models from the shelf. The name Discovery was painted on the side of the shuttle and was an exact replica of the photos she'd seen of the real thing. How many hours had he spent constructing this? An image of a young Christopher carefully gluing together the pieces made her smile. Before any damage could come to it, Sara replaced the model and grabbed a handful of empty clothes hangers.

Behind her, the bedroom door opened and closed as she hung up her robe. "She won," Christopher said sounding like a little boy who'd just been told he couldn't go out and play with his friends.

Sara closed the closet door and turned around. "She's the one that has to do all the work. If she doesn't mind neither should you."

Christopher frowned. "I guess. I just wanted to make it easier for her. There's no need for her to do it all."

"I was going to wait to tell you, but since you look like you need some cheering up I'll tell you now." Sara moved closer to him. "Last week Governor Campbell contacted me about coming to work for his administration. " Sara continued referring to the governor of California. "I accepted the position on Monday. Starting next month, I'll be a California resident." As much as Sara loved living in DC, she hated being so far away from Christopher. So far they'd managed to make things work by visiting each other on weekends but every week it got harder and harder to part again.

Instantly Christopher's face lit up. "Why didn't you tell me?"

"I wanted to surprise you." She brushed a light, gentle kiss across his cheek.

"Goal accomplished," he said with a laugh. "I guess that means you'll be looking for a place to live."

"Any suggestions?" She wanted to move in with him, but she didn't want to ask.

Christopher wrapped his arms around her. "How about with me?"

"I hoped you'd ask," Sara admitted, wrapping her arms around his neck and showing him just how much she loved him.

Coming Soon Book 4 in
The Sherbrookes of Newport Series

Now read ahead for a sample from A
Highland Heist a contemporary romance
by Cali MacKay

A Highland Heist

By Cali MacKay

Chapter One

On all fours, Maggie ignored the footsteps coming up behind her, with no more than a fleeting thought to her rear end which was sticking up high in the air as she struggled with a stubborn bolt, the front half of her body wedged behind the wood paneling. Her fingers cramped as she felt around to try and loosen the connection, working blind in the near dark of the enclosure. Nearly there... and then the last of the stuck bolts twisted free. She finished and pulled herself out of the opening in the wall only to find her new client standing there with another man at his side.

Perfect. She hauled herself to her feet and dusted her hands off on the legs of her jeans, trying to ignore the raised eyebrows on her client and the analytical look of the stranger, whose eyes drifted past her face to somewhere just above her head. Casually, she reached up and tried to smooth her hair. Uncontrollable to begin with, it seemed to have picked up a miscellany of cobwebs and dust. She managed to keep her groan from escaping. Nice first impression.

Iain MacCraigh's lips quirked into an amused smile. "I'm sorry to be bothering ye when ye're working, but I wanted to introduce ye to Conall Stewart. He's in charge of computer security for all my businesses and home, so ye'll need to integrate the work ye'll be doing here on the museum with his existing systems."

So, this was the computer genius Iain had mentioned. She wasn't sure how she felt about having a stranger involved in her project, but at least he was good—really good. Not one to leave things to chance when it came to her work, she'd researched Conall thoroughly after Iain first told her they'd be working together, and she was impressed. Not an easy thing to do.

She considered herself to be at the top in her field, and if she was going to be stuck working with him, then at least he knew what he was doing. As a woman in the male-dominated field of high-end security, she was damned if she'd have her hard-earned reputation damaged by working with someone who wasn't up to snuff. And she sure as hell wouldn't risk the Highlander's Hope, a treasure of priceless value. The system she was putting in for the museum Iain was building would incorporate her most advanced designs and equipment.

With a smile, Maggie shook Conall's hand as she took him in, her gaze wandering over his handsome form. There was certainly something about the man that had her pulse kicking. "It's a pleasure."

His hair was just long and wavy enough to have a mind of its own, the color of it like honey and aged whisky. Yet it was his eyes that held her attention. A warm amber flecked with gold and chocolate, lit from within with a fire and intelligence. He was tall and well-built for someone who sat at a computer all day, and his scruffy stubble made her want to reach out and run her fingers across his strong jawline.

This could be fun—except for the fact that the man looked far too serious for his own good. With luck, she'd get him to pull the stick out of his arse. Life was too short to not take full advantage of all it had to offer—a lesson she'd learned the hard way.

Conall mumbled a half-hearted greeting in response, before giving Iain a quick glance. "I'd like to get started if ye don't mind. There's a lot to be done, especially if we're to have everything ready and in place for the New Year's ribbon cutting."

Iain turned to her with a consoling smile, his eyebrows flicking up in a way that said *better you than me*. "Well then… I'll not delay ye any further. If ye need me for anything, I'll be back at the house. Cat will be back later this afternoon, so don't be too surprised if ye find her snooping around. Good day to the both of ye."

Once Iain had gone, Conall stood there, his eyes locked on hers. "Maggie Brennan, aye? Twenty-seven. Head of Brennan Securities out of Dublin, Ireland. Co-founded with yer father, Liam Brennan, though he acts as more of a consultant. Ye graduated top of yer class from Trinity at the early age of eighteen, and have won several awards for yer innovative designs and inventions. Three younger brothers, one who works for ye. Unmarried, no children. And ye drive a motorcycle—far too fast if yer speeding tickets are anything to go by."

She crossed her arms in front of her chest, pinning him with an unwavering gaze, amusement fighting with the slight annoyance that wanted to rear its ugly head. So the boy had done his homework. Fair enough. But she was no gombeen.

Her lips tugged into a hint of a smile. "Conall Stewart... Twenty-eight. Founder and sole employee of Stewart Technologies. Graduated from MIT before returning back home to Dunmuir, Scotland, where you were born and raised. You're specialty is hacking into company networks to find their vulnerabilities so you can then reinforce their systems. Never been married, and ye have no sprogs. Parents are divorced, one younger sister. Ye live alone in a home you own outright, and ye drive your Audi far too slow—if your lack of speeding tickets are anything to go by."

"Hmph." He looked her over for what felt like a very long time, but she held her ground and his gaze. When he spoke, it was still with no humor, as if he was tolerating her because he had no choice. "Might as well get started then."

By the gods, serious as he was, she was going to love pushing his buttons. She grabbed her bag of tools and headed across the room, leaving him to follow as he would. She glanced over at him, a smile breaking through to the surface, unable to remain serious for long.

"So do ye always look like ye swallowed sour milk or is the pleasure all mine?" That got her a glare, and she had to laugh. "I'm just yanking your tail. Curious to see what ye might look like if ye actually smiled a bit. Bet you'd be handsome. Or are ye worried 'bout the wrinkles? They've got creams for that, ye know."

His mouth pursed into a thin line. "I'm here to work, aye? Not to socialize. So if ye don't mind…"

Her anger sparked and bristled just below the surface as she stopped and pinned him with an icy stare. Reminding herself that she'd be working with Conall for the foreseeable future, she bit back the sarcastic remarks that wanted to spew forth, and told herself to let it go, knowing she was overreacting.

She took a deep breath and forced herself to calm down a notch or two, though when she spoke it was through gritted teeth. "Just so we're clear—*nothing* gets in the way of my work. Nothing. Don't take my humor and amiable mood for disinterest or incompetence. It'll be a mistake you'll regret."

Was it... could it be? Her eyes must be deceiving her. A smile tugged at his lips. "I've no doubt ye could make me regret many a thing, lass. Now if we could get back to work—please—I'd greatly appreciate it."

If she were being generous, she might even take that as a sort of apology. She grinned, her anger dissipating and her humor back. "Happy to oblige ye."

As they moved through the construction area, Maggie looked around at the progress being made. Though she was there to tackle the technical end of the security system for the museum, the bulk of the project fell to the construction crew who'd be transforming the old church ruins on the MacCraigh land, and rebuilding them into a museum that would house the Highlander's Hope and the paintings that had supplied the clues that enabled Cat and Iain to find the bejeweled necklace. There would be additional space reserved for items Cat planned to get on loan from other museums.

With the structural parts of the museum built, she and her brother were laying the foundation and wiring for the systems and tech they'd soon be installing. "With the electrical now in, we've run the cables that will support the final safeguards and security measures. We're using the most current tech so that any disturbances to the system will be detected —whether physical or over the net. If ye have changes you want made to the computer securities, I'm happy to work with ye so the systems run seamlessly."

Conall wandered, stepping over construction debris and tools, as his gaze took it all in. "I'll need to see yer security schematics and blueprints. Depending on how ye've set it up, there may need to be some changes made."

She sighed. This was why she hated having others work on her projects. As a security company, they were more than capable of handling the computer end of things, even if her specialty was creating security tech—complicated biometrics, motion and interference detectors, photoelectric scanners, and anything else her mind could dream up.

At least Conall was one of the best in his field. It only made sense that he'd want to look things over. He wasn't passing judgment on her work, but rather making sure everything operated at an optimal level.

She stepped to his side and looked up at him, liking how the sun streamed through the tall windows and gilded him in gold. "They're in my work trailer. If ye'd like to join me, we can go over them there. Or I could drop them off at your office."

"I work from home." He gave her his business card. "I'd like to see them now, but if you could also get me my own copy, it'd be much appreciated."

"I'll drop one off for ye later." She tilted her head with a smile. "In the meantime, follow me. My bus is out the back."

She led him outdoors to the RV she used when working away from home. It housed all her supplies and tools, and acted as a workshop, allowing her to make adjustments to her gear and tech without having to leave the worksite.

She'd had it custom made to her specifications, and then outfitted it further with her own tech. The vehicle itself had cost her a pretty penny, but it was a necessity when she was constantly away from home. It offered her a bit of familiarity and comfort in her ever-changing environment.

Letting them in past the safeguards, she climbed up the steps with Conall trailing right behind her. Though large and spacious for a bus, it was packed with equipment, forcing them to squeeze through towards the back where she kept all her plans and diagrams. There'd been larger models to choose from, but she hadn't wanted to run into problems while travelling down the tight winding roads once outside of the city. "Ye'll have to excuse the tight quarters. I think I over-packed for the job. Didn't want to need something and not have it."

With eyebrows raised, he glanced around, though his expression had yet to change much. "Do ye also sleep here?"

She could have laughed at the way he was eyeballing the place. It was clear he didn't care for the cramped accommodations. "I have in the past, but with this job scheduled to last months, I've opted to rent a place not far from here."

Paging through her blueprints, she pulled out the ones she needed and handed them to Conall. He laid them out on the table and took a quick look. "Do ye mind if I take these back to the museum?"

"Not at all. Just make sure I get them back before ye go, and I'd greatly appreciate it if ye don't leave them lying around—or show them to anyone, for that matter." He probably thought she was being paranoid, but she didn't care. She took plenty of risks in life—just not with her work.

His eyes narrowed with a glare. "Ye're not the only professional here, lass."

She beamed at him with a big smile, refusing to get into a pissing match. "Well, I'm glad to hear it. As soon as I dig out the blueprint printer, I'll get ye your own copy of the schematics and drop and them off. Now if ye don't mind, get out. I've got work to do."

His lips quirked into a smile. "Ye know, we may just get along after all."

❦❦❦
A Highland Heist by Cali MacKay is now available for purchase.

Made in the USA
San Bernardino, CA
13 February 2016